Step-Chain

All over the country children go to stay with step-parents, stepbrothers and stepsisters at the weekends. It's just like an endless chain. A step-chain. *Get Me Out Of Here* is the fifth link in this step-chain.

I'm Ed. I live in a madhouse. Believe me, it's true! What with the twins playing their pretend games, Alice screaming and Phoebe hassling me, I don't get a moment's peace. In fact things have got so bad I think I might go and live at Mum's. That will show them all. But is it what I really want? Life's a bummer!

Collect the links in the step-chain! You never know who you'll meet on the way...

Step-Chain

GET ME OUT OF HERE

Ann Bryant

EGMONT

First published in Great Britain 2002
by Egmont Books Limited
239 Kensington High Street
London W8 6SA

Copyright © 2002 Ann Bryant
Series conceived and created by Ann Bryant
Cover illustration copyright © 2002 Mark Oliver

The moral rights of the author and cover illustrator have
been asserted

Series editor: Anne Finnis

ISBN 0 7497 4822 2

3 5 7 9 10 8 6 4 2

Typeset by Avon Dataset Ltd, Bidford on Avon, B50 4JH
(www.avondataset.co.uk)
Printed and bound in Great Britain by
Cox & Wyman Ltd, Reading, Berkshire

CONTENTS

Step-Chain

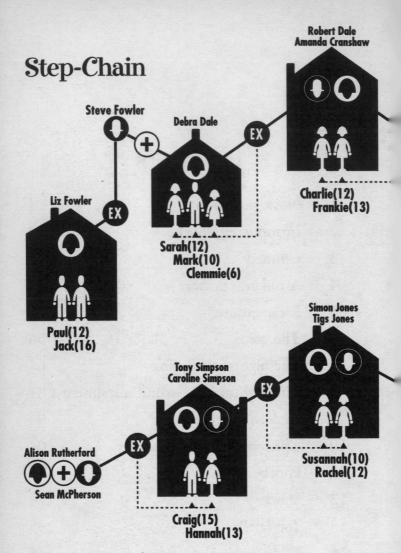

Robert Dale
Amanda Cranshaw

Charlie(12)
Frankie(13)

Steve Fowler

Debra Dale

Liz Fowler

Paul(12)
Jack(16)

Sarah(12)
Mark(10)
Clemmie(6)

Simon Jones
Tigs Jones

Susannah(10)
Rachel(12)

Tony Simpson
Caroline Simpson

Alison Rutherford
Sean McPherson

Craig(15)
Hannah(13)

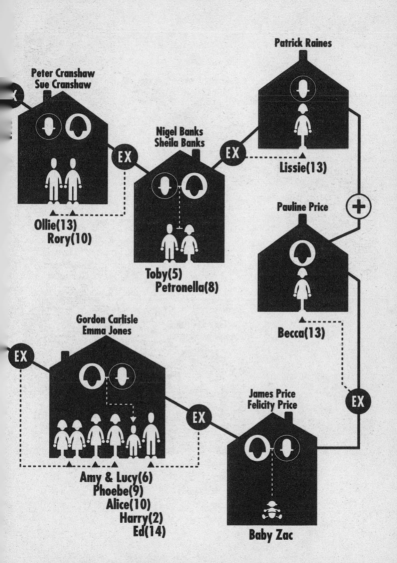

Read on to discover all the links . . .

1 NOISE POLLUTION

I don't know how much longer I can put up with the twins and their 'pretends'. They make up such rubbish, and right now they're spouting it just outside my bedroom door, which is getting badly on my nerves.

'Pretend I'm the train driver and whenever we stop you have to get off . . .'

'Yes, and when I get off, I click my fingers and a taxi comes along and I tell the taxi driver where I want to go . . .'

'Yes, and I'll quickly change into the taxi driver.'

'Yes, and you do the click because I can't.'

'I can't either.'

'*I* know! Pretend we're in a special place where they don't do clicks with their fingers. They do them with their tongues like this . . . *click click click (giggle) click click . . .*'

Oh God, this is driving me nutty! I'll have to tell them to shut up in a minute.

They were getting on some kind of weird six-year-old high, making loud train noises and doing high-pitched screams because they can't whistle. I blocked my ears because I know from experience that once my stepsisters get going, they don't stop till they've gone right over the top. I turned my radio up, but it didn't block out the whistling, giggling, screaming train outside my door.

Finally I snapped, opened the door and yelled, 'Shut up, you two!'

'Shut up yourself, Ed!'

I think that was Lucy. It's hard to tell the

difference between Lucy's and Amy's voices.

'Yeah, shut up yourself, Eddy Teddy!'

One of them giggled.

'Yeah, Eddy teddy bear, big fat pear!'

Massive explosion of laughter from both of them.

'Ha ha! Very funny indeed if you've got a brain the size of a pin-head.'

I doubt they heard that. They were both giggling hysterically. I slammed my door so they'd know there was no point in coming back at me with any more witty six-year-old stuff.

The whole house seemed to shake. I'm sure it's going to collapse one of these days. It's very old and pretty big. But not big enough for eight people. And that's how many of us there are.

In the playroom, which is below my bedroom, I could hear Harry bawling his eyes out.

'What's the matter, hmm?' Emma's sing-song voice came floating up.

I bet I know. My two-year-old half-brother is obsessed with this one particular toy. It's called Reggae Rattlesnake (I'm sure I never had any cool toys like that when I was his age. Life's a bummer!) and it's made of green and yellow coloured plastic and looks about as much like a rattlesnake as I look like Father Christmas. But still, there you go. The problem is that the on/off switch is a bit stiff for Harry and it really makes him mad when he can't work it.

Well, whaddya know! Emma's switched on Reggae. Bet I can guess what's coming next. Harry may have a problem with the on/off switch, but he sure knows where the volume control is. Any second now... Yup! He's turned it right round to top volume. So now the stupid piece of modern technology is snaking round the room, its tongue whipping in and out, while it plays this nerdy pop song with a clunky beat. Reggae might be one neat toy but the noise doesn't half get on your nerves, blasting up through the floorboards.

I turned my radio up to try to block it out. But nothing would block out what came next.

It's impossible to describe the *Omigod-I've-just-seen-a-spider* scream of my stepsister, Alice. Compared with Alice's scream, rattlesnakes and two-year-olds crying seem as soft as a mouse snoring. The scream is her trademark. She does it about fifty times a day – because, like I said, this is an old house, so spiders like to live here. I don't expect they find it quite so great once they've heard that bloodcurdling racket though. They probably turn to each other and say, *Quick, let's get out of here, guys. We've only picked a house with a monster living in it.*

'Ed! Where are you? Get this spider out of my room!'

At your service, ma'am.

I sighed, got up and made my way to Alice's room. I've learnt from bitter experience that there's no point in pretending I haven't heard her, because that girl is capable of yelling and screaming for up to an hour, and I'm the only person in this madhouse who doesn't mind picking spiders up (apart from Dad, and he's hardly ever here 'cos he's always at work).

Alice was cowering on top of her chest of drawers. 'It's gone under the bed now,' she wailed. 'You'll have to move the bed. I won't be able to sleep in here tonight if I think there's a spider under there.'

I gave her a withering look. She goes through this kind of spiel every time I move the stupid bed, which is about five times a week in spider season.

The poor old spider tried to run back into the darkness as its hiding place started moving, but I grabbed it like a professional spider catcher, and held it not too tightly in my fist.

'Ugh! Chuck it out of the window!' she yelled, pressing herself against the wall.

And that's when I suddenly thought, *Ed, you*

sucker. What does Alice ever do for you?

'Listen, Alice, it's time you got over this spider thing of yours.'

'I can't. I'm too scared. Don't bring it anywhere near me, Ed or I'll scream the place down.' (I believed her.)

'It's a poor defenceless spider, Alice. What's it going to do to you?'

'It's not that. Even looking at it makes me shudder.'

'But if you stop shuddering and think, you'll realise that you're being stupid, won't you?'

'You're the stupid one for arguing about it when it would be much easier just to get rid of it.'

For a ten-year-old she's got a lot of quick answers. And that wound me up even more. I think it was the way she sat there cowering and *still* gave me orders. I mean, I could have found a nice fat hairy spider and put it down her back. That would have been the quickest way to cure her of her spider phobia. Most of my mates'd do that to their sisters just for a laugh. Alice is lucky to have such a nice stepbrother as me.

'Look, Alice, just hold it. It's not like it's a big one or anything.'

'Mum!' she screeched. 'Ed's bullying me. Come here, quick! Mum!'

Good job the spider had got my hand round it to protect it, otherwise the poor thing would've keeled over from the noise pollution.

'Shut up, Alice. You're frightening it to death. Just try looking at it, then.'

I swear I only took one step towards her – OK, my fingers were uncurling, but very slowly – and she jumped off the chest like a power-crazed grasshopper, and landed in a kind of heap on the floor, clutching her ankle and screaming, 'You've made me break my ankle now!'

And that's when Emma – my stepmum, Alice's real mum – came in. She didn't look worried – just kind of frazzled and a bit tatty, same as normal. She'd tied her hair back in one of those big clip things but it was coming loose and bits of it were falling over her face. Harry was on her hip wriggling to get off. Whenever I think of Emma I picture her exactly like this.

She bent down to let Harry off, then started stroking Alice's ankle absent-mindedly.

'I had to jump off the chest of drawers. Ed was going to put a spider on me,' Alice told her, sobbing dramatically.

'That's cr- ubbish,' I said.

'Ed was going to say a rude word, Mum.'

Emma opened her mouth to speak but Alice got in first again with her high-pitched whine.

'Where is it now, Ed? You'd better not have let it go in here!'

I opened the window and chucked it out. 'There you go! Another one bites the dust,' I said, rubbing my hands. 'I'm going to ring the RSPCA about you, Alice, and report you for psychologically damaging innocent spiders, then making them risk their lives dropping from a second-storey window.'

Now the spider was safely out of the way, Alice made a miraculous recovery. She uncrumpled herself and stood up. 'It's not RSPCA, actually, Ed, because spiders aren't animals, they're insects. It's RSPC*I*, except that there isn't such a thing.'

She was giving me one of her smug looks with her chin sticking up, which gets to me almost as much as that scream of hers.

'Spiders are arachnids, not insects,' I told her calmly as I went out. 'So it *is* RSPCA.'

I saw Emma trying to hide a smile.

'Your ankle seems to be better now, Alice,' she quickly changed the subject. 'Come down with me and Harry. There aren't any spiders in the playroom.'

'Aren't you going to tell Ed off?' came Alice's sulky voice.

I didn't hear the answer to that because the sound of the phone ringing blotted it out. I went through to Emma and Dad's room and picked it up. We've got three portable phones in the house but we're always losing them.

'It's Tom.' (Tom never bothers with anything like 'hello'.)

'Hiya, Tom,' I said, grinning. I can't help grinning when I'm talking to my mate Tom.

'I'm in town.'

'Yeah?'

'Yeah.'

Phone chats with Tom crease me up. It was obvious he'd phoned to see if I could meet him in town, but he can't quite ask things directly.

'Have a medal!' I said, trying not to laugh out loud.

'What are *you* doing?'

'Not a lot.'

There was a long pause. This was even worse than Tom's usual telephone style.

'I'm in Our Price.'

'Oh, right.'

'Seeya then.'

I rang off and thought about the phone call. It was just as though someone was holding Tom at gunpoint and stopping him from saying what he wanted. I decided to go and meet him. Anything to get out of this place.

2 INTRODUCING PHOEBE

It was when I turned down Broomleigh Lane, which is a cut-through from our road to the main road into town, that I first got the feeling someone was following me. I'd heard a few noises behind me and thought it was just the wind. Only then the noises seemed more like a shoe scuffing or a jacket flapping.

Every time I heard anything I whipped round, but there was only a man in the distance. I began to think I was going mad. When I got to the end of Broomleigh Lane I could see all the way back to the other end and there was no sign of anyone or anything, so I *must* have been imagining it.

From here, for the next kilometre or so to the High Street, is a really busy main road. The cars zoom along it even though there's a 40 mph limit. Emma's cool about me going into town whenever I want in the holidays, as long as I tell her first. Alice isn't allowed to, so she's jealous. Sometimes she goes to her friends' houses, but they usually come to ours, as if our place isn't crowded enough already.

Coming from a quiet, neat little house with just Mum and Dad and no brothers or sisters, to the crowded, noisy place where I live now, was quite a shock, I can tell you! It was great at first because it all seemed so much more relaxed, and I could leave my room in a mess and no one told me off. I liked having loads of people around too – it was such a change. Then Harry was born – yet another person – and gradually my stepsisters started getting on my nerves. So that's where I'm at right now, which is how come Alice's friends drive me mad because they're all like Alice – really girlie and loud and giggly (and scared of spiders).

It was crowded in town. I went into Our Price. A quick scan round told me Tom wasn't in there so I went next door into Woolworth's.

'Hi.'

I turned round to see my stepsister, Phoebe, grinning up at me from underneath her baseball cap. It took me about three seconds to piece everything together. She makes me mad when she does things like this – which is most of the time.

'What are you doing in town, Phoebe? You shouldn't be here. You followed me, didn't you? I knew there was someone behind me.'

The grin grew bigger. She bent down to slap the velcro sticker back into place on her trainer. 'I'm a good hider, aren't I, bruv?'

I ignored that.

'Emma's probably going ape, Phoebe!'

'Bet she hasn't even noticed I'm missing.'

'Course she will have noticed by now. You're going to get killed, you know.'

'Nah, I won't.' She was fingering these soft toys with weird names like 'Groovy Chick' and 'Funky Bird'. 'Buy me one of these, Ed? I'll pay you back in two weeks.'

'Phoebe!' I hissed at her, turning her towards me. 'You don't seem to get it – you're going to be dead!'

'Phone her then.' She was looking at the toys again. But she had a point. I felt in my pocket for my mobile. No mobile.

'I've left it at home . . .'

'Tut tut, Ed. Memory like a sieve!'

Phoebe is nine. She sounds like she's sixteen at times. I don't know where she gets it from. She's such an off-beat kid. Nothing fazes her – absolutely nothing.

She was flipping through the CDs. I noticed a store detective with his eye on her. I wasn't surprised. I'd watch her if I was a store detective. She's got long hair but she always stuffs it inside a baseball cap. I wear one too, but at least I look normal in mine. She was wearing jeans that seemed too big for her spindly legs. She'd threaded a dressing-gown cord through the loops at the top of them. The ends of the cord dangled down the side of one leg. Her jumper was dirty but her trainers were glowing whiter than white at the ends of her jeans. I couldn't help staring at them, they looked so . . . big and bright.

'You're wearing Alice's trainers, aren't you, Phoebes?'

'Use Tom's phone,' she said instead of answering my question.

'It could take half an hour to find Tom . . .' *Click click* went my brain. 'How did you know I was meeting him, anyway?'

'I was in Mum's wardrobe.'

'What were you doing in there?'

'Hiding, 'cos I thought it might be Mum rushing to answer the phone.'

'But what were you doing in their bedroom in the first place?'

'Seeing whether I could jump out of their window on to the flat roof. I reckoned I could have done, but that's when the phone rang.'

'You're nuts, Phoebe! You could break your leg or your back, you know.' No answer. 'If you slipped and went over the edge, you'd be dead. So don't do stuff like that, OK?'

'Did you bring your wallet?'

I couldn't believe the kid! 'Have you heard a single word I've been saying, Phoebe?'

'Yeah, only I really want that Gritty Grace,' she said, back to fingering a hideous purple soft toy. I closed my eyes and considered strangling her.

'I haven't got any money, and even if I had I wouldn't buy you that.' The kid was acting like it was some kind of family outing. 'When's it going to enter your freakish little mind that you're not supposed to act like you're my age?' I marched her out of Woolies by grabbing her arm, twisting it round her back and pushing. The store detective gave me a funny look. He probably thought I was taking the mickey out of him, pretending to do his job. 'We're going to find Tom, then I'll phone Emma and you're going straight home. Get it?'

'There he is,' she said, pointing with her free hand. (Any other kid would have been gasping with the pain of the arm-lock. Not Phoebe.)

Sure enough, Tom was just across the road. But for a moment I thought my eyes were deceiving me, because the jammy bloke had only got his arm round a girl's shoulders. So that explained a few things.

'Tom's got a girlfriend. He's one step ahead of *you*,' said Phoebe. She was grinning at me, trying to wind me up.

'It's not a race,' I told her in my flattest voice, so's not to give her the satisfaction of thinking she'd rattled me. It was embarrassing seeing Tom like this. He's the last person I expected to get a girlfriend. Most girls take the mickey out of him. I yelled across the road, 'Oi, Tom, lend us your phone a sec.'

He moved his arm away from the girl to look round, trying to suss where my voice was coming from. Then the moment he spotted me, the arm was back. What a loser!

I shot across the road, clutching Phoebe's wrist tightly. The moment we got to the other side she yanked herself free and stuck out her hand to the girl.

'Hi, I'm Phoebe,' she said.

The girl looked as though she'd just landed on Jupiter and things were all a bit strange. 'I'm Izzy,' she said shakily. (Phoebe had given her the killer handshake. It was her idea of a joke to watch people wincing when she squeezed their fingers too tightly. A nine-year-old shaking hands! She is one weird stepsister!)

'Give us a lend of your phone, Tom,' I said, 'cos it was obvious he hadn't heard me the first time. Actually, I was quite pleased to have something to say so I could keep my eyes on Tom, because the girl was looking at me in this really wet way, like I was Robbie Williams or something. What was going on? I mean, why had Tom phoned me in the first place? Did he want to show off his new girlfriend or what?

'Run out of battery,' said Tom.

I groaned. 'Thanks a bunch, Phoebe. I'll have to take you home. Come on.'

Izzy was still staring at me. I could feel her eyes boring big holes in my face. Either I'd got a bogey hanging out of my nose or she fancied me. I couldn't think of any other reason for staring like that. Let's hope it was the bogey. I was going red just *thinking* she might fancy me because there was no way I fancied her. She was too young for one thing, even if she acted like she was seventeen.

'*We* don't mind walking back with you, do we?' she said. 'Where do you live?'

'It's miles away,' said Tom.

'The house with the great long drive on Firth Road,' said Phoebe. Izzy's nose was all wrinkled up as though she was trying to smell it from where we were. 'It's the other side of Broomleigh Lane,' Phoebe added helpfully. (Except she didn't *look* helpful. She looked as though she thought Izzy was a complete div.)

'Come on, Tom. Let's go,' said Izzy, sounding all excited, like she was off to Paris.

'I'll lead the way,' said Phoebe. She set off at about a hundred miles an hour, darting in and out of the shoppers.

'Slow down!' I yelled at her. I don't know whether she was pretending not to have heard me, or whether the traffic noise was too loud, but she wasn't slowing down. In fact the gap between us was getting wider every second.

'I'll have to catch her up,' I said to Tom.

'Seeya then,' he replied.

I think he was quite relieved because he didn't look too relaxed running with his arm round Izzy's shoulders. She'd got high heels on and a tight skirt, so her knees looked as though they were glued together, and her feet kicked up at the sides when she ran. What a sight! The two of them were kind of bumping against each other and going up and down at different times. I would have killed myself laughing if it hadn't been for the fact that when I turned back to Phoebe, there was no sign of her anywhere.

3 CONNED

Putting a spurt on, I felt myself getting madder and madder. I'd only gone into town to get away from Alice and the twins, and now I'd got Phoebe to sort out. She was going to pay for this.

When I got to the far end of Broomleigh Lane, there she was, leaning against this big old tree. She took the wind right out of my sails because I thought she wasn't going to be there. I'd imagined she'd be off hiding somewhere.

'Hiya, bruv,' she said with her trademark

grin. 'Took your time. Want to see my hiding place?'

I wasn't in the mood for her wit. 'No, I don't.'

She didn't seem bothered. She was looking back down the way we'd come.

'Hey look, there's Tom Tom the Piper's Son.'

I turned round. She was right. Only where was Izzy?

Tom looked red-faced as he got nearer and it was obvious he'd been running to catch me up.

'Where's Izzy?' called Phoebe.

'She had to go,' he said.

'Why?' asked Phoebe, grinning.

'Dunno.'

Something embarrassing must have happened. His face wasn't red just because of running.

'Wait here while I take Phoebe back to the house,' I told him. 'It won't take me a sec. Come on, Phoebe – race you.'

I knew that would make her put a spurt on. I even let her beat me.

'I've brought Phoebe back, Emma,' I called the moment we'd got through the back door.

'Where from?' asked Emma, sounding puzzled.

Oh great! She hadn't even noticed. I suppose when you've got loads of children, you can't be taking the register every twenty minutes. I couldn't be bothered to go through it all. I just wanted to get shot of the kid and go into town with Tom.

'Doesn't matter. Seeya then, Emma.'

'Seeya.' She still sounded puzzled. Poor old Emma. It must be quite a pain having to keep track of so many of us. Harry was the only one who was hers *and* Dad's. She'd had Alice, Phoebe and the twins with her ex-husband, Simon. Then there was me. When Emma and Dad got together, she had to get used to me and vice versa. At least she only had me to get used to – I had millions of stepsisters.

Maybe I've got a screw loose, living in this

madhouse. Sometimes, when everyone's driving me demented, I get to wondering what it'd be like living with Mum again. When she and Dad were together I never used to mind about tidying my room and having to take my shoes off the moment I walked in through the back door. I was used to it. I'd never known anything else. But whenever I go over there these days, which isn't very often, it's a hassle having to think about not messing anything up.

And then there's James, Mum's new partner, and their little burping baby, Zac. Well, basically, this is the score: I don't like babies when they're that little. I don't like people cooing over babies. I don't feel as though I know Mum any more and I don't particularly like James. So that's why I reckon I'm better off here with the screams, the crazy pretends and the rattlesnake.

Phoebe followed me out of the house.

'Izzy fancies you,' she grinned.

Please let her be wrong about that.

'Your mind's weird,' I told her.

But I had the horrible feeling she was right. How embarrassing. And then there was Tom. What was she was doing with him if she fancied me? Phoebe *must* have got it wrong.

'Hey, you've got my trainers on!' came Alice's loud voice from an upstairs window.'

Spotted, Alice!

'Spotted!' Phoebe called. (What is she? A mind-reader?)

Uh-oh! Here we go!

'Mum!' screeched Alice. 'Phoebe's nicked my trainers.'

'I borrowed them, that's all.'

'Well, you're supposed to ask before you borrow people's things, Phoebe.'

'Have them back. I've finished with them.' Phoebe unstuck the velcros and chucked them wildly up towards the window.

One of them landed on the flat roof, miles away from Alice's window, and the other one hit the house and fell down into a drain.

'Mum!' shrieked Alice. 'Look what Phoebe's done!'

Emma was nowhere to be seen, but Harry came tottering up to the open back door and swayed around in that kind of drunken way that little kids do, then fell out on to the doorstep. I didn't rush to pick him up because he was always falling over. As usual he stayed silent for about five seconds then yelled the house down.

Maybe I should take a rain check on living here.

Tom and I were walking towards the playing fields at the far end of town, eating crisps. I'd been wanting to ask him about Izzy ever since we left my place, but it was too embarrassing. I mean, this was my mate Tom!

There's Tom, Josh, Shane and me and we've known each other since primary. OK, it's a bit different at primary because if you're a boy you hate all girls, and you take the mickey out of them and don't let them join in your games or anything. When you get to secondary it's totally sad having a girl as a friend, unless you've made sure everyone knows that your mums are best friends or something. But in year eight and nine it starts to change. You don't have to do anything if you're a boy – the girls do it all. They kind of shout things across the classroom at you, and you have to think quickly what to say back to them, or whether to ignore them or what. If they think you fancy them and you don't, it's a nightmare getting rid of them.

Me and the others once bet who'd be the first of us to go out with someone, and everyone (except me) said *me*. So it was a shock to find Tom with his arm draped round someone's shoulders, when he hadn't given me any warning or anything.

Right, Ed – go for it!

'What school's she at?'

'Grammar,' Tom said.

'Yeah, so where'd you meet her?'

'Our Price.' (Why did I have the feeling that this was going to take a while?)

'What, and she just came up to you? Come on, Tom, what happened? Give it me in big-style detail.'

'She kept smiling at me when I was phoning you, and when I'd finished she asked who I was phoning and I said my mate and she said wicked and then she asked me if I was going out with anyone and I said no, and she said I could go out with her if I wanted.'

I couldn't believe what I was hearing. 'You big dur, Tom. No girl just comes up to you and asks you if you want to go out with them.'

'Yeah, I know.'

'You *know*! So what'd you say yes for, you doughnut?'

' 'Cos I didn't know *then*, did I?'

I thumped my fist against my forehead. It was like Tom had suddenly lost a load of slates.

'So how come you know now?' I said, trying to be patient.

' 'Cos when you went belting off to catch up with Phoebe, her friend suddenly appeared, like she'd been following us, and said something to Izzy about winning the bet.'

I couldn't help it, I creased up. In fact I had to stop I was laughing so much.

'Shut up, Ed. If you tell anyone, I'll tell your dad about that time you skived off.'

'What was the bet?' I managed to splutter out.

Tom was getting all wound up and his face was going red again. 'I'm not the only one she tried to con, you know! The friend said she'd seen another boy just up the road and it was *her* turn next.'

'Her turn to do what?' I'd stopped laughing. Now I was curious.

'To get a boy to buy her a Coke or something. That's what they do – see who can get the most boys to buy them drinks or whatever. She'd just said about going to Taff's Caff when you turned up. But anyway, once I'd clicked, I told her a thing or two. I said, "You might think you're clever, but I think you *look* stupid, you *sound* stupid and you *act* stupid, and you didn't win the bet because I never bought you anything." Then I just left them and went after you.'

'Good on yer! That told her.'

'You'd better not be taking the mick, Ed. It could have easily been you, you know.'

Tom was redder than ever, but it wasn't embarrassment this time. He was mad with himself because he'd been conned.

'OK, calm down. Let's go to Taff's Caff – see if anyone's in there.'

When we got there, Tom kind of hung back from the door.

'They'd better not be here,' he whispered,

rolling his eyes and looking mysterious as we went in.

They weren't. Well, not at that moment.

After we'd been in there for about twenty minutes and were both bored and ready to go, we caught sight of them outside. At first they were just standing there giggling, but then they came right up to the window and pressed their noses against it, shielding their eyes to see who was inside.

'Don't look!' said Tom, sucking his last bit of Coke up through the straw as though his life depended on it.

But it was too late. Izzy's eyes were looking straight into mine. And this definitely wasn't a *you've-got-a-bogey-hanging-down* look. It was so embarrassing. I pulled my chair round so I wasn't right opposite the window.

'What's *she* want?' I said to Tom, as if I didn't know.

'Don't ask me.' He looked at his watch and

his eyes goggled. 'Oh no! I've got the dentist!'

'When?'

'Ten minutes ago. Come on.'

The gormless girls had disappeared, thank God, so Tom went off one way and I went the other.

'We're going away tomorrow,' he called when we were about thirty metres apart.

Cheers, Tom. Thanks for telling me.

'How long for?'

'Dunno. Coupla weeks, 'spect.'

What a nutter.

The first thing I saw when I got home was Phoebe's head and shoulders sticking right out of Emma and Dad's bedroom window.

'Go back in, Phoebe. What did I tell you before?'

I sounded like her father. It was a real shame she was only nine. If she was fourteen like me we'd probably be best mates. As it is, it's a pain having to make sure she doesn't kill herself doing something crazy.

'Alice wants her trainer back and Mum says we've got to wait till Dad gets home. Come and look, Ed. I bet *you* could get it, no problem.'

The moment I went through the back door I heard the rattlesnake chonking away. Harry was in the passage between the playroom and the kitchen. He was trying to dance. His knees were bending and snapping and he was clapping and twisting at the same time.

'Nice one, Hal!' I said to him.

'Edededededed!' he said, changing the knee bends to quick stamps. He tried to follow me then burst into tears when I tore off.

'Pretend I'm only three and I can't say train, so I say *choo choo*,' came Amy's voice from the twins' room.

They were at it again. The 'pretends' they invented were incredible. If ever I have friends round I try to make sure the twins aren't within earshot because I don't want anyone to think I've got a couple of loonies for stepsisters.

'Hurry up, Ed!' called Phoebe.

'My trainer's going to be stuck there for ever if we wait for Dad to come back,' said Alice, appearing from her room at the sound of my name.

She followed me into Emma and Dad's room, where Phoebe was crouching on the window sill. I hauled her off and leaned out to look. Alice leaned beside me.

'There it is. Up that end. I'm sure we've got a ladder. You could –'

She was interrupted by a familiar voice coming from down in our drive.

'Hi Alice!'

'Izzy! What are *you* doing here?'

Oh g-reat!

4 AVOIDANCE TACTICS

'Aren't you going to invite me in then?' the stupid kid called in a sort of breathy voice. She was looking at *me,* not Alice, so I got a pretty big clue why she'd turned up out of the blue at our house. She'd also conveniently got rid of her friend, I noticed. But surely she didn't think she could try it on with me like she had with Tom? I didn't get girls, I really didn't.

'Don't expect *me* to have anything to do with her,' I said to Alice as we left the bedroom.

'She's come to see *me,* you wally!'

There was still a nano-chance that I might have got it wrong.

'Is she one of your friends, then?'

'No, I hardly know her. She's in the parallel class.'

My palms were sweating. This was unbelievable! 'The parallel class! What! Are you saying the kid is the same age as *you*?'

'A few months older . . . But she's one of the cool ones. She probably got bored at home or something . . .' Alice started to look a bit panicky. 'Can you let her in, Ed, while I phone Ellie and Justine? I don't know what to say to Izzy on my own.'

'I'm not letting her in!' I squeaked, and bolted for my room.

About twenty minutes later the doorbell rang (so Alice must have let Izzy in then got straight on the phone to her two best friends, Ellie and Justine). I could hear all four of them talking as they went past my room.

So now they were safely in Alice's room, but there was no guarantee they were going to stay there, was there?

Don't be pathetic, Ed. She's only a stupid little primary school kid, for God's sake. Maybe she fancies you or maybe she's trying to con you like she did Tom. Either way, you just ignore her. And if you come face to face with her you just give her one-word answers and plenty of evils.

Sorted. I moved the chair away and opened the door as quietly as I could. Even with Alice's door shut I could hear them talking about clothes and make-up. Alice sounded like she'd aged about four years. It was obviously laid on for the great Izzy.

'I'd never wear anything but dark blue or very dark red on my toenails. It said in my magazine that pale colours are out.'

I got a horrible shock when Izzy changed the subject.

'D'you get on with that dreamy brother of yours, Alice?'

'Nah, not really.'

Oh 'scuse me while I go and puke. I went downstairs and out of the back door like a rat down a drainpipe. The twins were in the bit of the garden that runs down the side of the house. It's their favourite place. There are loads of shrubs and a little shed that's getting pretty crumbly because half the wood's rotten and some of the tiles are missing. This is where they play their most way-out pretend games.

Right now they were behind a nearby shrub. Lucy was speaking.

'*I* know – pretend you have to follow me wherever I go and if I say *What do you want for tea?* you say *Leaves* or something . . .'

'Yeah, 'cos I'm an alien,' said Amy, looking dead keen. 'And if you say *willow tree* I say . . . *willy pee!*'

They both collapsed in hysterics, so they didn't notice me go past them.

I'd decided to go round to Josh's to see if a miracle had happened and he'd come back from his holiday three days early. Anything to get away from this house.

'Ed!' I stopped in my tracks. 'Can you get my trainer now?'

I turned to see Alice and the others coming out of the front door.

Great timing, Alice. Thanks very much.

'I'm going to Josh's.'

'They're not back till the weekend. Zoe told me.'

Yeah, thanks again, Alice. (Zoe was Josh's sister.)

'You only need a ladder,' said Izzy in this really gooey voice. She was looking at me like I was Superman. If this was all part of the big con, she was a pretty good actress.

Alice, Ellie and Justine shot Izzy a look as

though they couldn't believe their ears, then they all stared at me. I suddenly knew what that poor little maggot felt like when I'd examined it under a microscope in science last term.

'We haven't got a ladder, actually,' I said.

'Yes we have, Eddie,' said Amy.

Oh wonderful! The twins had joined the enemy front line now.

'*I'm* not scared of heights, Ed,' said Izzy. 'I don't mind going up there if you hold the ladder steady for me.'

She looked a real twit standing with her hand on one hip and batting her eyelashes. Even the twins were staring at her.

'It's nothing to do with being scared of heights,' I said in my hardest voice.

'So why don't we get on with it?' she replied, all sweet and sickly. 'Come on, Alice, show me where the ladder is.'

Then Emma appeared in the doorway in the nick of time.

'Can one of you help me for a while?'

Saved!

'Actually, Alice and her friends were just saying how bored they are,' I quickly said. 'They'll help.'

Alice shot me a daggers look.

'We never did!'

'I just need someone to watch Harry while I make a couple of phone calls,' Emma said.

'Oh yes, let's play with Harry,' said Justine. 'He's so adorable, Izzy. You'll absolutely love him!'

So Izzy was dragged off with the others. I couldn't help smirking.

But my smug feeling fell on its bum with Alice's next words.

'It'll be great when you come to my sleepover on Saturday, Izzy. We always have lots of fun, don't we, Justine?'

No reply. Justine had rushed on ahead to get to Harry first.

Izzy was the last to go inside. In the doorway she turned and treated me to another of her revolting smiles. Now I was sure this was no bet. She was trying too hard. She fancied me. What a bummer. I swung round and strode off. I didn't know where I was going and I didn't care.

Almost out of earshot I stopped in my tracks at the sound of Amy's voice.

'*I* know – pretend I'm that big girl with Alice, and you're Ed, and we love each other.'

They both giggled. I nearly threw up.

5 ESCAPE ROUTE!

It was Thursday night. Dad and I were watching telly in the kitchen and Emma was clearing away round the sink. Correction – Dad was watching telly. I was doing what I'd been doing for the last half-hour since Alice had gone to bed – staring at the screen and planning how to tell Emma and Dad what I'd decided. OK, it was no big deal – I only wanted to spend the weekend at Mum's. Well, I didn't exactly *want* to, but I'd had to think of something drastic to make sure I wasn't anywhere near that Izzy kid.

It was a while since I'd been to Mum's. Emma and Dad knew I hadn't enjoyed it at all the last time, so it was pretty likely I was in for a bit of the third degree once I made my announcement. They'd probably both look at me in this kind of searching way, and say, *There's nothing wrong, is there, Ed?* I hate it when grown-ups do that. It's like they've just been on a counselling course and they think they're the most understanding people in the world, with some kind of line through to children that no one else has got. And you just want to say to them, *Look, can we cut the amateur psychology bit? I really don't need any sympathy, you know.*

Right, here goes!

'Dad . . .'

His eyes never left the screen. Actually, now I was looking at him, I saw that his eyes were nearly closed. He's always tired in the evenings. Emma says his job's too stressful. She wishes he didn't have to commute so far every day.

'M-hm?'

'I wouldn't mind going to Mum's for the weekend . . .'

The droopy eyelids instantly sprang to life and he looked at me as though I'd said I wouldn't mind going to Mars for the weekend.

'Oh . . . right.'

Emma came and sat down at the table. She was still clutching the J-cloth – a dead give-away, that!

'I thought you didn't like it last time, Ed.'

'Yeah, I know – but I was just thinking it'd make a change. You know . . .'

'Yes, of course,' said Emma, nodding at Dad as if to tell him not to dig any deeper on this one.

'Well, that's . . . fine,' stumbled Dad. 'Do you want to give your mum a ring then?'

Trouble is, I never know what to say to Mum on the phone. I can't just launch in and ask if I can stay.

'Can you do it, Dad?'

'Yes . . . all right. What shall I say – the whole weekend?'

Not necessarily. Just from five minutes before Izzy walks through the door until five minutes after she goes.

'I was thinking of Saturday afternoon till Sunday afternoon – something like that.'

That should cover it nicely.

'Well yes, that's fine as far as we're concerned, isn't it, Emma?'

'Absolutely. I expect Zac'll be sitting up by now,' she added with a smile.

My heart was beating faster than usual while Dad tapped in the number for Mum's. Why? It was only my mum, for God's sake. But then again, who was I kidding? Emma's more like a mum than my real mum is. We're totally relaxed with each other. She gave me loads of hugs when I had chickenpox last year, and that's when I realised I was completely used to having her around. She'd never had chickenpox herself, and Dad kept warning her that she'd catch it if she got that close to me.

'If I catch it, I catch it,' she'd said, and she'd leaned forwards and given me a big sloppy kiss like she was deliberately going against Dad. She'd been holding a mug which still had some honey drink – her 'magic potion' – in it, and it spilt on my duvet in a big sticky pool.

'Now look what you've done!' Dad had said, half-smiling, like he always does when Emma does silly things.

And Emma had just laughed and gone for a cloth. If that had been Mum, all hell would have been let loose because of messing up the duvet. It was nice the way Emma wasn't bothered. Nothing fazes her about the house.

'Felicity, it's Gordon,' said Dad, going for his jovial telephone tone, even though he and Mum don't get on at all. They went through a few polite questions and answers, then Dad said,

'Ed would like to come over this weekend. How are you fixed?'

There was a long pause while Mum was talking at the other end and Dad was frowning and nodding at the floor. I started to get worried in case it wasn't convenient for me to go over there. Dad covered the mouthpiece and looked at me. I knew immediately that it was a *no*. 'Mum and James are going out on Saturday evening, Ed. It's something they can't rearrange easily.'

'So? I could babysit Zac.'

'They're taking Zac with them. It's a party. They're going to put Zac to bed and stay the night. What about next weekend? Mum says that's free . . .'

Next weekend isn't the weekend that I need an escape route for, thanks all the same, Mum.

My mind was going into overdrive, trying to think what to do now. It had never occurred to me that Mum would say no. I shrugged and got up to make a drink.

'We'll ring you back, Felicity. Ed's not sure what he's got on next weekend.'

There was silence after Dad put the phone down, but I bet he and Emma were giving each other loads of looks behind my back.

'Mum sounded very sorry,' Dad said.

'Really?' I said, without bothering to turn round from the kettle.

There was another silence apart from the spoon rattling as I stirred my tea.

'So we'll fix it for next weekend then?' said Dad, smiling at me like I was about six and a half as I came back to the table.

'It'll be a relief to have a break from the madhouse, eh?' Emma added, with exactly the same over-the-top smile.

'I'm supposed to be going to Josh's next weekend,' I said, coming out with the first thing that entered my head. I'd only taken about two sips of tea, but I left it and got up. ' 'Night.'

* * *

The following morning I had a brainwave. I bet Shane would be around. I went straight down to the living-room to use the phone.

'Hiya, Shane. What are you doing?'

'Nothing much . . . I'm grounded.'

Uh-oh! Could be a problem.

'How long for?'

'Till Monday.'

'Are you allowed to have friends over?'

'Doubt it.'

'What if you ask?'

'Mum's not talking to me. She might do later. I'm going to wash the car and mow the lawn and grease up to her all morning.'

'Wicked. Then can you ask her if I can stay over at your place on Saturday night?'

'Yeah, I can always try . . . Don't you want to know how come I'm grounded?'

Shane then told me this great long story about staying out two hours late. I tuned out long before he'd finished. I was trying to work out what to do if his mum said no.

About an hour after I'd rung off, the phone rang and I snatched it up thinking it would be Shane. It wasn't. It was Mum.

'Hello, Edward love. I never know who's going to answer in your house!' She laughed. It suddenly seemed odd the way she called it *my* house – like she was making it quite clear I had a separate life from hers. 'Had a bit of re-think, Edward. James and I would love you to come over. There's no way we can cancel on the Greenhalghs' at this late stage, but we could pop over there for a little while if you'd like to look after Zac?'

Her voice was all bright and crisp. I didn't like it. And when she said the name, James, loads of old feelings came back. I can still hear the sound of his horrible posh voice arguing loudly on the phone with his ex-wife about their daughter, Becca. Mum must have been mad to want to be with him.

What was I thinking? There was still time to change my mind. I could pretend something else had come up, couldn't I? But then I'd have to suffer Izzy . . .

Right on cue Phoebe came into the living-room.

'Talking to your girlfriend, Ed?' she grinned.

That did it.

'Thanks, Mum. That'd be great.'

6 THE VOICE

Emma drove me over to Mum's. She'd brought Harry with us so Dad could get on with putting up shelves in the twins' room. The twins stayed behind to watch Dad and pretend to be 'builders', but Phoebe and Alice had decided to come along for the ride. As usual, the car was very full and noisy, but today it was worse than ever because Harry had insisted on bringing his Reggae Rattlesnake.

Mum and James moved into a brand new house about six months ago, and Alice had never seen it before.

'Is that their house?' she asked as we pulled up. 'It's very . . . clean, isn't it? Not like ours.'

'The subtle difference is that ours is old and this is new,' I told her.

'It's still very clean,' Alice shouted above the noise of the rattlesnake.

'Can you switch that thing off, one of you?' said Emma.

Harry promptly started wailing.

'Can't you give him a sweet or something, Mum, to shut him up?' said Alice.

'No, I'm not getting into that habit.'

'You have to sing to him, that's all,' said Phoebe.

She broke into *Daddy's Takin' us to the Zoo Tomorrow* and Harry instantly cut the dramatics and stared at her with this weird lopsided smile on his face, like he was hypnotised or something. I sometimes think Phoebe's got magic powers. There's definitely something witchily odd about the kid. When she started clapping in time with the beat, Harry did the same. Then when she pretended to be a monkey *scritch scritch scratching*, Harry copied perfectly. It was such a funny sight.

'Ed do!' he cried excitedly. So I did – just for a laugh!

'Alice do!' he then said.

'No, I'm not pretending to be a monkey!' said Alice, folding her arms and looking superior.

'Well, *I* will!' said Emma. And when Alice realised she was the only one not joining in, she soon started scratching away like a pro.

By the time Phoebe had sung that verse three times we all knew the words – even Harry. And it was when we were belting out the chorus at top volume that a shadow fell across the car. I looked out of the window to see James standing there, with a puzzled expression on his face, holding Zac. We must have looked like a family of complete loonies.

One by one we all stopped singing except Harry, who couldn't care less about looking a fool. Emma got out of the car.

'Hello,' she said, going over and poking Zac in the tummy.

Zac just stared.

The rest of us got out of the car, except Harry, who was still singing and scratching away. Zac looked completely different from the last time I'd seen him. His face had got bigger and squarer and his hair had grown.

James put on this really silly little high-pitched voice, like he was pretending to be Zac answering.

'He-llo, Em-ma. He-llo!'

Still Zac just stared. It was all pretty squirm-worthy.

'How's it going, Ed?' James then said to me, in a *what a cool person I am* voice that I'd never heard him use before. He usually sounded much more stressed out and snappy. I was trying to suss whether he'd really changed or whether he was just pretending to be laid back in front of Emma.

I mumbled 'OK, thanks,' but he wasn't listening. His eyes were on Phoebe's dirty bare feet. We're all used to Phoebe and her ways. We know she hates all shoes except trainers. As she'd lost her own – and couldn't wear Alice's, because Alice was wearing them – she'd abandoned footwear altogether. But James was probably wondering what kind of a family I lived in.

'D'you want a hold?' he said to Alice, offering her Zac.

'No thanks,' said Alice. 'I've had enough of babies.'

James looked embarrassed, which was nothing to the way I was feeling.

'Where's Mum?' I asked.

'Ah . . .' His eyes started shifting about. *Yeah, let's hear the excuse for why my mum can't be here to greet me when she hasn't seen me for about two months.* 'She's had to pop into town to get prezzies for the Greenhalgh children. I guess she's got caught up somewhere . . .'

There was a silence. Even Harry stopped banging on about bears *huff huff a puffin'*.

'We'll be on our way, I think,' said Emma. 'Come on, you two. In the car.'

'Have a nice time, Ed,' said Alice.

'Hang loose,' said Phoebe. (That's what I used to say about a year ago.)

'See you tomorrow,' said Emma, squeezing the top of my arm, like she does.

Then off they all went, and I felt as though I'd been dumped on a planet where there was no life.

James put on his strange voice, which was half 'baby' and half 'person talking to baby'. He thrust his lips right forwards so he was practically kissing Zac. 'We take Ed in the house now? Hmm? Is that what we do, Zacky? Yes it is . . . yes it *is*!'

Then Mum rolled up in her gleaming red Fiesta and I've never felt so relieved to see her in my life.

'Who's dat?' said James in the Voice, shifting Zac round so he could see Mum getting out of the car. 'Who's dat, hmm?' Zac kept up his trademark stare. 'It's Mama, isn't it? Hmm? Can you say Ma-ma? Ma-ma?'

Oh, shut up before I puke!

'Sorry, Ed . . . Hello, my little sausage!' She was rubbing noses with Zac. James handed him over and then – shock horror! Mum handed him to me.

'I bet you've noticed how much he's grown,' said Mum. 'It's not so obvious to us because we see him every day.' Then she made the same face as James had done, with her lips all sticking out, and asked Zac from point blank range if he could say Ed.

Don't be so pathetic, Mum!

Eventually we got inside and I was able to

escape the thrilling threesome and go to my room. It wasn't actually *my* room. It was the spare room (or the guest room, as Mum and James call it). It was so clean and tidy I felt as though just sitting on the king-sized bed would mess it up.

There was one of those tea-making things by the bed. On the wall above it was a picture of a woman in the nude. One of her boobs was up by her left ear. (I really don't get modern art.) The carpet was nearly white, and I reckoned it'd be some kind of miracle if it stayed that colour until I went. It had been a blue carpet the last time I'd stayed. Fancy having a brand new carpet after such a short time. Dad and Emma would probably keep the same carpets till they wore through to the floorboards. The bedspread had been changed too. It was white and pink.

I had my own bathroom. It was all shiny in dark red and (yup!) white. Every little bottle and tube was in its place, the carpet was smoothed down and the rug was fluffed up. I'd never seen anything like it. I'd go mad if I had to live here.

When I got down to the kitchen, Zac was in his highchair with a clean white bib round his neck. Mum was running her finger along a row of baby food jars in the neat orderly cupboard. The sink gleamed. The floor shone. I'm sure she was never this much of a motherly housewife when I was little. I reckon James has made her worse.

'Just feeding Zac. It won't be long till his bath and bedtime.'

She smiled at me then made a funny face at Zac, as James came in and asked Mum crossly where she'd put the newspaper.

Here we go. Back to your usual snappy self, James.

'It's in the magazine rack, isn't it?'

'I have actually looked in there, Felicity,' he replied semi-sarcastically.

'Do you want me to feed Zac or look for newspapers?' Mum asked, giving him an evil. I didn't like the way this conversation was going.

'I'll feed Zac if you want,' I offered, like a good boy.

'Thank you, Ed,' said Mum, flashing me an over-the-top smile, then scowling at James as if to say, *You see,* some *people round here are nice and thoughtful.*

I yanked open the jar she was holding, grabbed the spoon out of her hand and sat down next to Zac. They both frowned at the jar. Was I supposed to pour it into a bowl? Tough!

It looked like the weekend was going to be a non-stop party. Still, at least I wouldn't have to suffer Izzy. And it didn't look as though Zac would be any problem. Once Mum and James had gone out, I could watch telly all night.

Little did I know . . .

7 THE NIGHTMARE BEGINS

''Bye, Ed. We won't be late, I absolutely double promise!' said Mum from the living-room door. 'Do go to bed if you feel tired. Only take the intercom with you, then you'll still hear Zac if he wakes up – not that he will, because he never ever does, but just in case . . .' She stopped and frowned. 'Now . . . is that everything? Oh! Silly me! Telephone numbers. Now – my mobile is written beside the phone in the kitchen, James's is by the phone in here, and I'll just –' She was grabbing pen and paper as she spoke – 'make a note of the Greenhalghs' number. There we are!'

'Felicity . . .' James appeared in the doorway, gave Mum an impatient look and tapped his watch. 'I don't know why you're bothering with all that. Zac's good as gold at night-time.'

I watched through the front window as the car pulled away. When it was finally out of sight it was one big relief. I felt like doing something a bit dodgy to celebrate. Explore! That would be a good start. So I started with the drinks cupboard – or cabinet, as James called it.

Sherry, Martini, vodka, whisky, another sort of whisky, gin, brandy, what's this? Courvoisier, tonic, more tonic, Bacardi, bitter lemon . . . Blimey, James, no lager?

I went through to the kitchen and found loads of wine, and cans of lager in the fridge. There were two baby bottles of milk in there too. Mum had bunged a pizza in the oven for me and told me to help myself to whatever else I wanted, but she hadn't said anything about lager.

Ten minutes later I was sitting on the floor in front of the settee, eating pizza and drinking lager. This is great! I wish I could phone Tom . . . But he won't be there. Maybe I'll try Shane.

No sooner had I tapped in his number than I dropped the phone like it was burning my fingers, because I distinctly heard a dog yelp right behind me. At first I thought I must be going mad. James and Mum hadn't got a dog. They'd never dream of keeping a dog. It would leave its nasty doggy hairs on the nice clean carpets. I must be drunk. OK, I'm not used to alcohol, but there's no way three mouthfuls is going to make me hear imaginary dog yelps, is there?

I tapped in the number again, and exactly the same thing happened. I found myself staring at the phone like a right twit – I mean, phones don't make dog noises. What's going on here? The third time it happened it went on a bit longer and sounded more like a baby than a dog, and that was when I clicked. Dur! It was the intercom.

The intercom! I nearly shot through the ceiling. Zac was crying. That meant he'd woken up. Mum said he definitely wouldn't wake up. And she must have been one hundred per cent sure about that or she would have left me with pages of instructions. I hadn't the faintest idea what to do. But one thing was certain – no way was I going to phone Mum. I didn't want her and James coming back and ruining my nice evening, looking all hacked off because I couldn't even babysit properly.

I crept to the settee and sat down slowly and stealthily. If I could hear Zac, could Zac hear me? As long as I just sat there, nice and still and silent, with any luck he'd go back to sleep.

Who was I trying to kid? For one thing the telly was blaring away in the corner, and for another thing Zac's yelps had stopped sounding like a dog, and started to sound like a baby crying its guts out. I couldn't ignore him much longer. I'd have to go up and face the music. I was about as prepared for this as I was for climbing Everest.

I tiptoed into his room, my heartbeat louder than my footsteps. He was thrashing about wildly, legs kicking for England. When he saw me he stopped crying, but then he must have cottoned on that it was me and not Mum or James, and his bottom lip trembled. Oh God . . .

'Hello, Zacky,' I tried, nearly making myself sick because it had come out sounding like James at his ultra-gooiest.

That did it! Zac's face went pink and he started yelling.

Am I supposed to pick him up or what?

I said a couple more soothing things in the Voice, which had no effect whatsoever, so I went towards the cot feeling like I was approaching an escaped king cobra in the High

Street. I got him out and jigged him about a bit but he didn't stop crying. I tried showing him stuff in the room.

'Look, Zac! Mobile! Tinkle tinkle! Good, isn't it?' (Didn't work.) 'OK, listen to this then!' I was tapping the wardrobe . . . 'Tappety tappety tap tap tap!' Then the window . . . 'Chink chink!'

The crying was louder than ever and he was all red in the face. Clearly my sound collage wasn't going down too well. Right – *think*, Ed!

Nappy! That's what you do to babies, isn't it? You change their nappy. Sorted!

First I had to find where Mum kept her nappy supply. I put Zac back in his cot. Big mistake that. The yelling grew so loud and gulpy that I thought he was going to choke or something. I quickly took him out again and miraculously he went completely quiet, just like that! His thumb went into his mouth and he snuggled into me, all hot and damp.

I felt pretty proud of myself, I can tell you. I

reckoned he liked me a lot. Maybe I wouldn't even have to change his nappy now. Rocking him (like a professional nanny, I might add), I walked over to the window. I was imagining Mum and James coming back and asking me if everything had been all right. I'd tell them casually that actually Zac had woken up yelling his head off, but I'd got him back to sleep, no problem. That'd impress them.

'Look, Zac – car.' I was pointing to Mum's red car parked outside. It was beginning to get dark but you could still easily make out shapes.

Well, that did it. He took a deep breath and went berserk. He laid into my chest with his fists, arching his back and kicking his legs.

'OK, forget the car. I mean it's only a car, Zac. It's no big deal, really. Or are you thinking it's one of those nasty machines that's whisked your mum and dad away, and left you all on your own with me?'

I put him on his back on the floor because I'd

spotted the nappies right next to the cot. But he instantly rolled straight over on to his tummy, and lay there kicking his legs with his head thrust forwards like a cocky tortoise. I put the nappy on the carpet next to him and went for a brisk efficient tone of voice, to show him who was boss round here.

'Right, here's the deal. You keep quiet and stop rolling over and kicking, and I'll sing you a song . . . Sounds pretty fair to me. Here we go . . .

> '*Twinkle twinkle little Zac,*
> *Please just stay there on your back.*
> *Do not kick and do not cry.*
> *Soon you'll feel all nice and dry.*
> *Twinkle twinkle little Zac,*
> *Please just stay there on your back.*'

It worked! He was lying completely still, staring at me like I was a rock star.

Uh-oh! Spoke too soon. Zac broke into big gulpy yelps, then he snatched up the nappy and whacked it backwards and forwards, which made a great backing for his crying but didn't help *me* much.

'OK, you keep that one. But you forgot the deal, didn't you? Let's turn you over on your back. That's right. I'll get another one. No problem . . .'

Or *was* there? I was looking at the white all-in-one thing that he was wearing, wondering which bit I had to undo to get at the nappy. There wasn't much chance to find out though, because he rolled over again. Oh why didn't I pay more attention when Emma was changing Harry?

The crying noise was terrible. 'What will the neighbours think, Zac?' What did he care? 'OK, that's enough mucking about, mate. We are now going for a serious nappy change. Ready?'

I knelt down and sat him on my lap. Then I started yanking the press-studs apart, working down from the top. It wasn't easy with Zac squirming and kicking and still crying for England. He'd also drop-kicked his nappy half way across the room, which was impressive. 'Thanks for that, Zac!'

Finally I had to lie him down again, and that was when I spotted one of those plastic changing mats. Harry had had one of these, only much thinner than this one, and with bits of foam coming out of one end. Brilliant! Cracked it! Zac was crying because he wasn't used to the carpet.

Once he was on the changing mat I realised that both the nappies I'd got ready were out of reach and so was the bag. I'd got my hand on Zac's tummy, but I was stuck.

'OK, we need to strike another deal, mate. I let go of your tummy and you stay still as a statue. This time it's more important, because you're not going to like it if you roll right off the mat, I can tell you.'

1,2,3, go! I took my hand off Zac's tummy for a micro-second while I lunged for the nearest nappy.

'Right, kid, this really *is* it, this time.' Even though his legs never stopped kicking I managed to get the white all-in-one thing off, undo the tabs on the old nappy and yank it out from under his bottom. It was saturated. 'Blimey! No wonder you were screaming the place down, Zac. *I'd* be a bit hacked off, and all, if I was soaked in wee like that.'

And that was when I had this vague memory of Emma rubbing some sort of cream on Harry's bottom before she put the new nappy on. I could see a bag of coloured cotton wool balls, which looked like bottom-dabbers. There was a big tub of something right next to them, so that must be the cream. Wicked.

Zac was much calmer now.

'See! Big brother knows best!' I felt right back in the driving seat again. This babysitting thing was a piece of cake. Zac was staring at the ceiling, not making a sound. What a relief! No need for my lightning grab-the-nappy technique. Just reach over calmly for the cream and cotton wool. Easy! Everything's under control.

I lifted his bottom up by holding his feet in one hand and pulling upwards, the way I'd seen Emma doing it. It worked brilliantly. Then I shoved the new nappy underneath, feeling pretty confident I'd got it the right way up, and got a big dollop of cream on my fingers. I was all set to rub it in when Zac did something mega-impressive. He weed in the air in a great big arc. I couldn't believe how high he made it go. Trouble was, it came down all over the new nappy.

'Nice one, Zac!'

Or . . . maybe not? Half the wee had landed

in a little pool and was soaking into the white carpet. Mum would go spare if her nice clean carpet had a big wee stain in the middle of it. Tell me this wasn't happening . . . I rushed to the bathroom, grabbed the nearest (white) towel and raced back to Zac's room. Zac hadn't moved, thank goodness. Maybe he was getting ready to do a big poo. There was no time to lose. I scrubbed away at the patch, thinking how grateful Mum was going to be that I'd managed to save her precious carpet with my speedy action. The towel wasn't much cop at drying it, but it got the worst of it off and I reckoned the rest'd dry on its own by morning.

My fingers felt all sticky, but the big blob of bottom cream wasn't on them. Great! That meant I must have smeared it over something. Oh well, no time to think about that now.

'I'm sure your bum can manage without cream just for once, Zac.'

It was only when I'd finally got a clean nappy

on Zac that I realised his all-in-one thing was sopping wet too, so I had to set about searching for a new one.

I was not impressed. With every drawer of the chest of drawers that I looked through, I got a little bit madder. 'Thank you *very* much, Izzy! If it hadn't been for you I wouldn't be here in the first place! And I certainly wouldn't be talking to myself either!'

Just my luck – not an all-in-one thing in sight. Oh well . . . 'You don't mind what you wear, do you, Zac?'

No answer. And better still, no crying!

It took me quite a while to get Zac dressed, but he looked really wicked in a Disney T-shirt and a pair of green dungarees, even if they were about three sizes too big for him. I laid him down on his back in the cot.

'Night night, Zac! Watch the bugs don't bite! Do us a favour and keep the noise down, mate.'

He just stared at me, so I went out. I was all

tensed up, waiting for one of those little yelps as I crept downstairs. Incredibly nothing happened so I went back to my lager and telly. I decided to forget about phoning Shane because that was what I was doing the last time the yelping started, and I didn't want to tempt fate.

About five minutes later, when there was still not a sound from the intercom, I began to relax. Zac must have gone to sleep. Like I said – piece of cake, this babysitting thing!

Oh yeah, Ed?

8 THE NIGHTMARE –
SECOND INSTALMENT

Piece of cake? More like a lump of gristle.

Zac gave me ten minutes to get into the film that had just started, then he broke into another big bout of gulpy sobbing. No warning at all. One minute it was silent, the next, all hell was let loose.

Maybe it was time I phoned Mum? She'd left me half a phone book full of numbers to ring, after all. But what would happen if I *did* phone? I could just hear her voice . . . 'I can't understand it. He never wakes up in the evening!' They'd rush home and I'd have to put up with James giving me sneery accusing glances like it was *my* fault their precious baby had woken up. Then Mum would go up to Zac, and James would watch telly with me.

No – no way was I phoning. I'd rather have a screaming Zac than a sneering James.

OK, so what do you do to babies apart from change their nappies? Give them bottles. Right. This time I was going to be smart. I'd get the bottle ready, then bring Zac downstairs and let him drink it while I watched the film.

In the kitchen I looked round for a bottle then remembered that I'd seen two in the fridge. Nice one!

I got one of them out and went upstairs two at a time, thinking how incredible it was that such a big noise could come out of such a little kid.

'Come on, mate.' I scooped him out of his cot without any mucking about this time. 'We're going downstairs, you and me.'

When I jogged down Zac started chuckling. Looking at his face was like looking at the sky when it's raining but the sun's shining at the same time and you know there's going to be a rainbow somewhere. He was all blotchy from the crying, with two bright pink spots on the top of his cheeks, but his eyes were crinkled with laughter and there was this big wide grin underneath.

We sat down together and I shoved the teat in his mouth. At first he looked as though he was going to really enjoy it, but in no time at all he turned his head away and this disgusted look came over his face.

'What's up, Zac?'

I tried once more.

Forget it. He was lashing out again, all fists and feet. 'Right, you're not hungry. I've got that. So what's the problem?' I didn't want to miss any more of the film so somehow I had to get him back into that chuckling mood.

'Come on, Zac!' I had a sudden burst of inspiration.

While he laid into me with both feet I jogged upstairs and sure enough the crying stopped. I jogged down again and the chuckling started. Brilliant!

'OK, everything's all right, Zac. So now we go and quietly watch the film. Deal?'

We sat down on the settee and five seconds later the crying started again. I let it go on for about a minute, but I couldn't hear the telly at all. Maybe if I jogged on the spot that would have the same effect as jogging up and down stairs. So that's what I tried, but for some unknown reason, Zac wasn't impressed. He didn't quieten down at all.

'OK, one more time.'

I set off upstairs, and hey presto! The crying stopped. I jogged back down again. Zac chuckled away. So *this* is baby humour! Let's take the rip out of big brother Ed. Good job

Tom's not here to see me making a fool of myself. I went into the living-room, sat down and . . . off he went again.

This was getting beyond a joke. What was I supposed to do? Spend the rest of the evening jogging up and down stairs? I'd be half dead by the time Mum and James came back.

I racked my brains to think what Emma would do to shut Harry up. Well it was obvious, wasn't it? She'd just switch on Reggae Rattlesnake. Why didn't I think of the obvious?

'Where are your toys, mate?'

There wasn't a single toy in sight and I couldn't remember seeing any in his bedroom either. Weird! They must be hidden away in a cupboard somewhere. I opened the tall cupboard by the telly and – result! It looked like it was full of every toy known to man.

I pulled out loads of them and scattered them all over the floor, then plonked Zac down in the middle. He rolled straight on to his tummy and started kicking and screaming the place down. I was getting more than a bit cheesed off. 'Surely you like *one* of these toys?'

One at a time I got hold of them and wiggled them round in front of him, but he just kept crying his eyes out. Time to put the brain into overdrive. Perhaps he'd done a poo. I had a quick sniff but there was no pong at all, and I wasn't about to change him again if I didn't really have to. Maybe I should leave him for a while and see if he quietened down. He couldn't get any louder, that was for sure.

After ten minutes my nerves were suffering big style. I couldn't hear the telly at all and I'd completely lost track of the film.

I had another shot at the bottle, but Zac practically knocked it across the room he was so keen to show me how much he hated it. So then I tried sitting him on my lap and giving him another exciting demo of every single toy.

By this time his face was so red it looked like

it was about to explode. There was nothing for it – I'd have to go back to Plan A and kill myself jogging up and down the stairs until Mum and James got back. I looked at my watch. Ten-fifteen. Oh no! Spare me!

On the way up, the crying stopped, true to form. I waited for the chuckling to start on the way down, but Zac must have got sick of this game, because he started wailing and howling like a sick wolf. I sat down on the bottom step and felt like joining in. It was then that the phone rang. With Zac clinging to me, hot, wet and noisy, I answered it.

'Hello, Edward, it's Mum.' Her voice changed. 'That's not Zac is it? My God, it is! Whatever's the matter with him?'

You tell me, *Mum.*

There was something about her voice that got to me. It was a mixture of worried, accusing and suspicious. I could just imagine James at her side, saying, 'What? What's wrong, Felicity?'

I wasn't about to tell them I'd messed it up.

'No, don't worry. It's the telly...' I zipped into the living-room and put Zac on the floor then went back into the hall and stood where I could see him kicking and arching. 'There, I've turned it down.'

'That's a relief!' Mum laughed. 'Although I knew it couldn't be Zac really. I was just phoning to check everything's all right and to tell you we're on our way back. Little Timmy Greenhalgh seems to have gone down with some virus or other. He's in quite a state. We'll be home in about ten minutes.'

Ten minutes! *Ten minutes!* Omigod! You're going to be sussed unless you think quick, Ed.

'Well, actually Zac did wake up earlier but I gave him one of his bottles and he went straight back to sleep.'

'Oh!'

She sounded so shocked, anyone'd think I'd given him Scotch on the rocks and just told her he was lying unconscious in his cot. It really got to me, that did.

'Oh!' she repeated. Seemed like I'd rendered her speechless. I just wanted her to give me a clue about what to do with the kid, but I was more determined than ever that she wasn't going to find out I'd had any problem. Mum regained her powers of speech a moment later. 'That was sensible of you, Edward. Though I suppose you're used to heating up bottles for Harry, aren't you?'

Bingo! You have to heat it up! No wonder Zac thought it was rubbish. But how do you do that? In the microwave?

'Yes, we use the microwave at home.'

'Uh-huh.'

I heard James mumble something in the background. Probably telling Mum to wind it up.

'Right, Edward, see you soon then.'

I was right.

'Yeah, 'bye!'

I shot into the living-room, grabbed the bottle, raced into the kitchen, put it in the microwave, counted to ten and took it out. I knew it only had to be warm, not hot, but it didn't feel any different from before. I put it back in, counted another ten, a bit more slowly, took it out and tried to visualise Emma with a bottle. Of course – you have to shake a few drops on to your arm to check it's not too hot, don't you? Perfect.

'Come on, mate. This is the one.'

I scooped him up, sat down on the settee, put the teat in his mouth and started praying.

Instant silence, apart from squelchy sucking noises.

We have lift-off!

I had eight minutes to get him tucked up in bed and hide the evidence. Better be on the safe side and hide the lager too. I kept an eye on my watch. Three minutes had passed by and the level of the milk had hardly gone down at all. The squelchy noises were getting slower. Come on, Zac. You can do better than this. Maybe he wasn't that hungry. He looked pretty much out for the count. I tried gently easing the teat out of his mouth but he instantly started sucking like his life depended on it. I waited a few seconds then tried again. Same thing. By the fourth attempt he was hardly sucking at all. He was totally zonked. Good job – I'd just heard the car pull up outside.

Toys were scattered all over the living-room and evidence of the nappy changing was all over Zac's room. OK, I could pretend playing with Zac and changing him had been such a cinch, that I hadn't bothered to mention it. Mum'd probably be really impressed with me. Right, all I had to do was get Zac into his cot.

One last deal, mate. Do not under any circumstances wake up!

I got up with as little movement as possible,

letting Zac carry on sucking, then I went upstairs as smoothly as an electric chair lift. I placed him carefully in his cot and very very gently took the bottle out of his mouth. The key turned in the front door. Uh-oh! The bottle was still warm. What a giveaway! I shoved it under the cot and legged it downstairs, breaking into a stroll at the bottom.

'Hi. I've just checked Zac. He's fast asleep.'

James's eyes were darting everywhere, as though he was looking for evidence of a disaster. Well, he wouldn't find any.

Mum turned to him and smiled. The look on her face said, *See? I told you Edward would be fine.*

'No problems?' Mum asked me as she went upstairs herself.

'Nah,' I drawled. It came out a bit more casually than I'd intended. 'No, everything's been fine.'

James looked amazed. Good. Missing the

film and the lager, worrying, dabbing, jogging, singing, making deals – it had all been worth it just to see the look on his face. *Huh! Gutted, James?*

9 BACK TO THE MADHOUSE

'Wasn't it much good, Ed?' said Phoebe.

I ignored her. Emma gave me a sideways glance. 'I expect it seemed a bit quiet after our noisy place?' she said.

It was getting on my nerves, this post-mortem. I mean, they'd only picked me up three minutes ago. I didn't feel like talking – well, not to them anyway. I just wanted to listen to my CD in peace.

'Did you miss me, Ed?' Phoebe said, leaning forwards so she could shove her grinning chops right in front of my face.

'Desperately!' I told her, swiping my hand in the general area of her head to get her off my case.

'Sit back and do up your seatbelt,' Emma told Phoebe. Then her voice softened for me. 'I bet Zac's better behaved than Harry.'

We were getting dangerously near the very subject I most wanted to avoid.

'He's OK,' I mumbled.

'Did the babysitting go all right?' Emma went on. 'I thought about you, all on your own with a baby.' She shot me a sideways grin. 'Or is he one of those babies that goes to bed and stays asleep all night?'

'Mm.'

'He's lying,' said Phoebe, who was right back in my face again. 'I can always tell when you're lying Ed, because you've got this bony thing on your jaw and it wiggles about.'

She reached forwards to touch and I lashed out a bit harder than I'd meant to. Being

Phoebe she didn't start moaning like Alice would have done. Normally Emma would have told me not to be so rough, but she let it go. I guess she was feeling sorry for me because she knew I was fed up. The bottom line is that Emma knows me much better than Mum does. I put my earphones on and listened to my CD with my eyes closed so I didn't have to suffer any more question-and-answer sessions.

For the rest of the journey home I thought about all that had happened.

I'd gone straight to bed the moment Mum and James had got in, so I wouldn't have to suffer any interrogations about my wonderful evening. Lying there wide awake, I'd heard them whispering in cross hisses though, so I knew I wasn't going to get off lightly.

I was right. This morning I went into the kitchen to find Mum feeding Zac.

'Morning, Edward,' she said, all tight-lipped.

'Morning, Ed,' said James in the same clipped tone.

So this was it.

'I saw you tried changing Zac,' Mum started.

Tried?

'Yes. He was sopping wet.' Her lips went into an even tighter line. What had I done wrong? It must be the clothes. 'I couldn't find any of those all-in-one things.'

'Hmm . . . and the nappy leaked during the night because you didn't fasten the stickers properly. I wouldn't have minded that so much if there hadn't been a big stain on the carpet, a white towel covered in wee in the middle of the carpet, a bottle of *warm* milk under the cot and baby lotion all over the door handles.'

'Not to mention a can of lager lying on its side under the settee and a big pool of lager beside it,' James chipped in.

I must have kicked it over without realising. Typical. Mum and James were both wearing the same *I'm sorry but we don't tolerate such sloppiness in* this *house* expressions on their faces. They made me sick. Even Zac was eyeballing me accusingly.

Come back, my crazy family – all is forgiven!

I looked coldly at Mum. 'You said he definitely wouldn't wake up. I was the one stuck here trying to get him back to sleep. Thanks for all the appreciation.'

James looked furious but Mum eased up a bit.

'I know I said he doesn't usually wake up, Edward, but I don't understand why you didn't phone me.'

James joined in then. 'Your mother could have told you exactly what to do, or we might have decided to come home even earlier, then things like that stain would have been avoided.'

Is that all you care about – a stupid stain?

I gave James my hardest look. 'I was trying not to disturb you actually.'

Mum came straight back at me. 'But why on earth didn't you at least say something when I phoned or when we got home?'

I didn't have an answer to that one, which made me mad, so I just shrugged. I was staring at the wall because it seemed a better idea than looking at either of them. I bet they thought I was a *right teenager*, but I couldn't care less.

After breakfast we went for a walk and came across some friends of Mum's and James's, who were also pushing a pram. They invited us round for coffee and talked about babies for a good two hours, while I was stuck in front of a video of *The Lion King*, like a little kid.

While Mum was making lunch and James was playing with Zac I had nothing to do. I tried talking to Mum, but it didn't really work. I had to keep thinking what to say, and what Mum *wanted* me to say, so it felt completely unnatural. When I'm with Emma, I can just say what I want and I don't have to think at all. It was weird that Mum was my mum and Emma was my stepmum. They acted like it was the other way round. Mum was so sort of polite with me – apart from this morning when she'd dropped the politeness to be cross.

Next I tried joining in playing with Zac, but because James was there too, even that felt funny – like I was acting a part. I just wanted to get back home to Dad and Emma and the rest of the madhouse.

At about three o'clock I said I ought to be getting back so I could see Uncle Trevor and Auntie Debs before they had to go. (Nice invention, I thought.) Mum must have been mega-relieved because she even offered to take me back herself, but then she added that it would have to be after four-thirty when Zac woke up from his afternoon sleep.

Not likely! I'm already bored out of my skull. No way can I stick it out till after four-thirty.

'That's OK, I'll phone Dad,' I said quickly.

Dad was watching the football on telly so that's why Emma had come for me, only she'd left Harry at home. Alice and the twins hadn't wanted to come, apparently, which suited me fine.

And now we were nearly home. Wicked!

I unplugged the seatbelt as we went up the drive, which is quite long and winding. Tom told me that when he first saw it he was expecting to find a massive great castle at the end of it. Then all he saw was a big old house, and he felt really disappointed. (Cheers, Tom! I'd told him.) I thought about that every time I came up this drive. Our house was so cool with its overrun garden, especially after that pristine place of Mum's.

The moment I was out of the car the twins appeared at my side. Lucy reached up and pulled me down by yanking an arm round my neck. It seemed like she was going to give me a kiss, which wasn't like her at all. Then when her face was level with mine she put on this really grown-up voice and looked at me like she was in love with me.

'Oh Ed,' she drawled, 'I've missed you.'

I needed reminding of that stupid Izzy like I needed toothache.

'Very funny, Lucy. Get off me!'

'No, she doesn't talk like that. Let *me* say it!' said Amy, trying to push in.

I grabbed my bag and followed Emma into the house. Phoebe came behind. The moment we got inside we heard Harry crying.

'Oh great!' I said under my breath. 'It's as bad as Saturday evening.'

'So you *did* have a problem with Zac!' said Phoebe, skipping in front of me with a triumphant look on her face. 'I knew you were lying in the car.'

I was waiting for Emma to tell her to shut up and leave me alone, but Emma's mind was on other things. Dad had come out of the living-room to meet us. He was carrying Harry and he looked quite worried.

'He's been moaning and whimpering like mad. I took his temperature in the end. A hundred and one. Is that bad?'

I hadn't been back thirty seconds and already there were signs of chaos.

Chaos versus order. Which is better? No contest. Give me chaos any day.

10 THE TERRIBLE ANNOUNCEMENT

It was Wednesday morning and I was on the phone to Josh when Phoebe popped out from behind my curtain as I disconnected. She was wearing cut-off jeans, with the dressing-gown cord still threaded through the loops at the top. The baseball cap was back to front so her hair was hanging in straggly bits round her shoulders.

'Can I come with you, Ed?'

'Have you been listening in on my private conversation?' (I don't know why I bothered asking – it was pretty obvious she had). 'You've got such a cheek, Phoebe. Can you get out of my room, please.'

'I'll stick my trainers on.'

'Oh, you've found them, have you?'

'No.'

She was off like a shot – probably to nick Alice's. I'd already heard how Dad had managed to get the left one down from the roof and Alice had fished the other one out of the drain, then Emma had put them in the washing machine. They'd shrunk a bit because Emma had then dried them by sticking them on the cylinder in the airing cupboard. Alice had gone ballistic.

'Right, let's go,' said Phoebe, appearing at my door twenty seconds later. (She was wearing the trainers. Would she *never* learn?)

'You're not coming with me, Phoebe. Get that into your head straight away. Emma!' I hoped Emma would be able to find something for Phoebe to do, which wouldn't involve her getting on people's nerves. Not easy. Phoebe would rather hang out with me or play tricks on Alice.

'Ssh!' said Phoebe. 'Mum's asleep. She was awake in the night with Harry again.'

Harry's high temperature turned out to be a virus. Emma had big rings round her eyes because she was so tired. She'd been up with Harry for three nights on the trot now.

'When she wakes up, tell her where I've gone,' I said as I pushed past Phoebe and ran downstairs.

'Alice!' Phoebe called out loudly to the house in general. 'When Mum wakes up, tell her Ed and me have gone to Josh's.'

'Shush! Now *you're* the one who's going to wake her up! And you're not coming. The end.'

I went out of the front door. Phoebe followed me. I set off jogging down the drive. Phoebe jogged behind. This kid was doing my head in. I stopped and swung round.

'Go back, Phoebe. I don't want you and neither does Josh.'

'Zoe might be in. I can hang out with her.'

'But what if she's not?'

'We could always phone and ask.'

I pulled my mobile out and tapped in Josh's number because it seemed the fastest way to get Phoebe off my case.

It turned out that Josh's sister *was* in, but she'd already got a friend round and she didn't really want Phoebe too. I knew Phoebe would try and come along anyway, so I was in a no-win situation. I reckoned it would be better to get Josh to come round to my place instead. At least that way there was quite a chance that we wouldn't be stuck with Phoebe hanging around the whole time. She'd soon get bored and go off and pester someone else.

When Josh turned up we went straight up to the attic, which is full of rubbish, but it's also got a dartboard.

'Can I play? I'm good at darts, aren't I, Ed?' Phoebe said the moment she saw where Josh and I were heading.

'Get lost, Phoebe,' I answered, because I wouldn't like it very much if Josh's little sister kept pestering to join in. Anyway, Josh and I had stuff to talk about. I wanted to tell him about how Tom got tricked by an eleven-year-old girl. I wasn't going to mention that the stupid girl had got a thing about *me*, though.

At one o'clock Alice came out to tell me lunch was ready. Josh and I had spent ages playing darts, then we'd played football.

Josh said he had to go because his aunt was picking him up and taking him to a leisure centre that afternoon for his cousin's birthday treat. Lucky thing.

'Have you seen Phoebe?' Alice asked.

I shook my head.

In the kitchen, the twins were helping

Emma. I was expecting her to look half dead because that's how she always looks right now, so it was quite a surprise to find her singing as she dished up the shepherd's pie. Harry was happy too. He was sitting in his highchair, banging his spoon on the tray and grinning round at everyone.

'Looks like Harry's better,' I said.

'Yes! Isn't it wonderful?' Emma smiled. 'I feel as though I've come out of a black tunnel.'

Alice came in. 'I can't find Phoebe. I've looked in most of the rooms and all over the garden. And I've called out that lunch is ready about a zillion times.'

'See if she's in your room,' Emma said to the twins.

'I bet she's hiding somewhere to try and get us all worried,' said Alice. 'That would be typical of Phoebe.'

'It's like there's not enough trouble in her life, so she has to go along looking for more,' I said.

Emma shook her head slowly, wearing a sort of Phoebe's-a-bit-eccentric-but-so-what? smile.

'Why don't we just start?' said Amy.

'Yes, and bad luck Phoebe!' said Lucy, turning both palms up and looking round at everyone with big eyes, as though she'd just said something important at a committee meeting.

'I expect she'll be here in a minute,' said Emma. 'You know how much she loves food.'

Normally Emma would be more concerned than this, but it was as though Harry was better so nothing else mattered. Personally, I reckoned the longer Phoebe kept away the better. It was great not to be pestered for once.

It wasn't till we'd got on to the pudding that Emma suddenly seemed to think there might be a problem after all. 'When was the last time anyone saw Phoebe this morning?'

'When Josh came,' I said.

'She came in our hut-house, didn't she, Amy?'

'When was that?' asked Emma.

'Ages ago.'

'What about you, Alice? When did you last see her?'

'About an hour ago when she came to ask me if I'd got Izzy's e-mail address.'

Uh-oh! 'What did Phoebe want that for?' I asked.

'Think she wanted to send her an e-mail.'

'Brilliant deduction, Alice. You ought to be a detective when you grow up.'

Alice smiled. She didn't get my sarcasm.

'When's Izzy coming to our house again?' asked Lucy.

'Dunno,' said Alice. 'Sometime soon, I expect.'

And that's when Phoebe strolled in.

'Where've you been?' we all chorused.

'I didn't know you'd started,' said Phoebe. 'Hope you saved me some. I'm starving.'

She slid into her chair while Emma put a plateful of shepherd's pie into the microwave.

'So where *were* you?' Emma repeated.

'I went down the drive.'

'She's got a den,' said Lucy smugly.

'How d'you know about that?' snapped Phoebe.

'We saw you in it,' said Amy. 'It's a tree.' She was looking at Emma, knowing that she was stirring.

'I hope it's not dangerous,' said Emma, in her I'm-warning-you voice.

Phoebe shook her head because her mouth was crammed with shepherd's pie. For a thin little kid she hasn't half got a big appetite.

'I'll check it out after lunch,' said Emma. Then she cleared her throat and said, 'First I've got something to tell you all.'

Instantly we all sat to attention. Even Phoebe stopped chewing and stared at Emma with her cheeks pouched out. There was something in

Emma's voice that told us this was going to be an important announcement.

'I'm going back to work.'

'What about Harry?' said Alice, in a little shocked voice.

What about all *of us?*

'I'm getting a childminder.'

It felt like she'd kicked me in the gut. Emma working? How bad would *that* be? She'd start wearing make-up and smart clothes and having neat hair and high heels. She'd click briskly about the place, organising everyone. Then next thing she'd get a cleaner and the house would be all tidy and pristine. It wouldn't be like our house any more. It would be like – it hit me hard – like Mum's.

As for a childminder, I could just imagine it. Phoebe would run rings round her, Harry would cry all day long, Alice would have rows with her and the twins would make up 'pretends' specially to wind her up. She'd never manage to keep everyone under control like Emma does. And who'd finish up having to dive in and sort it all out? Yours truly.

G-reat!

11 PHOEBE GOES TOO FAR

It seemed like I was the only one who was bothered about Emma's big announcement. Maybe the others hadn't worked out that things were about to change.

'Come on, let's go and look at this den of yours,' Emma said to Phoebe after lunch.

I decided to join the inspection team.

'That's it,' said Phoebe. We looked up. There were just two old sheets hanging down way up high. 'Watch.'

She swung herself up to a low branch, then stood on it. Emma and I stood right next to the tree trunk because it was the only way to see her. She reached up for another branch and swung herself up on to that one. It was pretty hairy stuff for a nine-year-old. I couldn't help being impressed.

'Well, I call that dangerous, Phoebes,' said Emma. 'You're very high up.'

'What's the point of it?' I asked her. 'What are you actually doing up there?'

'Just being here. It's my den. Watch this then.'

In about three seconds flat she dropped down to the lower branch, then swung herself right out and jumped to the ground. Unfortunately for her she landed in a patch of nettles. Any other kid would have screamed the place down. Not Phoebe. She just found a dock leaf nearby and rubbed her ankle, while she grinned up at us.

'Good, isn't it?'

'Well . . .' said Emma, 'I'm still not sure. I'll speak to Gordon.'

'OK,' said Phoebe, swinging herself back up.

'Eddy Teddy, it's for you,' said Amy, rushing out of the house just then, holding the phone like it was a gun.

Both the twins were grinning, which set a few alarm bells ringing. I snatched it, went into the house and straight into the only place you could get any privacy – the loo.

'Hello.'

'Hi! It's me.' Izzy. I recognised her voice instantly and my heart sank. Who did she think she was, calling herself 'me'? Anyone'd think we phoned each other every day. 'Can you talk?'

Well, I'm not dumb, am I?

'Uh?'

'Obviously not. Don't worry, I'll do the talking. I've got Alice to invite me over again this weekend, so we'll be able to see each other. I can't wait. I'm only phoning because I wanted to hear your voice. You can get the rest from my e-mail . . .'

E-mail! That did it. I didn't bother with ''bye', just disconnected and legged it up to my room. There are two computers in this house and I've got the one with the Internet and e-mail. I connected and waited.

Receiving message 1 of 1

And there it was. Omigod!

> *Dear Ed,*
>
> *Thanks for your lovely e-mail. Don't worry. I understand about you not wanting Alice to know what you think about me. She IS a bit stupid, isn't she? (Giggle giggle.) We agree on so much, you and me. If I'd seen you first, I never would have done nothing with your mate Tom. Honest. See you at the weekend. I can't wait. We should be able to lose Alice, no probs, like you said. I'll be there at about 5. Only three days. Hugs and kisses, Izzy.*

My head felt dizzy and my hand was shaking as I went into *Sent Items*. There was Phoebe's e-mail that she'd sent to Izzy, pretending to be me. She'd had plenty of time to get in here while Josh and I had been playing darts. As I read it, I felt my face growing redder and redder.

> *Dear Izzie,*
> *Alice dose'nt no this, but I am very in love with you and allways have bin ever since I set eyes on you when you were with Tom that time.Im not telling anyone about thes feelings Iv got because there personel. Don't tell Alice about this e-male because it woud be embarasing. Any-way I don't rekkon she'll find out because shes quite thick. Not like you. Ive tried asking Alice to invite you to come over, only she says no. If you phone and ask, shell probly let you. Then we can see each other with-out anyone noing. Goodbye for now. Big smoochy kisses*

and hugs from your Eddy teddy. !!!!!!!!

I went like a stone from a catapult downstairs, outside and down the drive.

'Phoebe!' I yelled at the top of my voice. 'You're dead!'

She wasn't there. Typical!

I raced back into the house and went straight up to Alice's room.

'You might knock, Ed.'

'Has Izzy phoned you and asked to come over?'

'Yeah.' Alice put on her sullen look with her chin in the air. 'She's my friend. I can invite her to come over here if I want. Mum said it was all right.'

'Yeah, well I'll soon put a stop to that.'

'You can't un-invite someone when you've already invited them, you know, Ed. Anyway, you can't phone now. She won't be there.'

'How do you know?'

'She's gone to her granny's and she's not coming back till Saturday afternoon. Then she's coming straight over here.'

'Where's Phoebe?'

'Haven't seen her.'

'The little . . .'

I stomped into the playroom to ask Emma where Phoebe had got to, but Emma flapped her hand to shut me up because she was reading a letter with a big frown on her face. Harry started tottering after me as I went back out again, then burst into floods of tears when he couldn't catch me. I went out to the twins' hut-house to see if Phoebe was in there. She wasn't. And neither were the twins. I was going back in when suddenly the twins shot out of nowhere and held hands round me, so I was trapped.

'Leave me alone, you two,' I said as patiently as I could. 'I'm trying to find Phoebe. It's very important.' *I've got an urgent appointment to kill her.*

'This is the Magic Circle,' sang Amy in a voice like an opera singer's. 'And we are the magic children from the Golden Wishing Well.'

'What is your wish, oh boy?' asked Lucy in the same voice.

'I wish you'd let me go,' I said quickly.

'We can only make *big* wishes come true,' sang Amy.

'OK, I wish I could fly,' I said, thinking that was pretty smart because then they'd let me go so I could fly. *Ha ha.*

'We can only make wishes a bit smaller than that come true,' Lucy warbled.

That did it. I tried to force their hands apart but they were stronger than I thought and when I finally managed it, they joined up again.

'That's enough, you two! Stop mucking about!' Emma shouted from the landing window. 'Let him go!'

'Where's Phoebe?' I asked her.

'I've just walked her over to Josh's sister's.'

That kid was too clever for her own good. She'd fixed it so she could be out of the way while I went ballistic. She was going to be such a challenge for a childminder. And as for the twins . . . if Emma hadn't been here just then, I'd still be stuck inside the Magic Stupid Circle when it got dark.

'Can you collect her later, Ed?'

With pleasure. I can throttle her at the same time.

12 SHOCKS

'Did you think I wouldn't find out?' I asked Phoebe through clenched teeth, the moment we'd left Josh's. 'That e-mail is full of spelling mistakes and it makes me look a total prat. And now Izzy is only coming over on Saturday. So cheers, thanks a bunch, Phoebe!'

She didn't say anything but she looked cross.

'I don't know why you're looking like that,' I went on. 'I'm the one who should be gutted.'

'Maybe you'll let me play darts next time,' was all she said.

I could hardly speak, I was so gobsmacked by her total cheek. 'You must be joking!'

That evening when Harry and the twins were in bed I re-read the pathetic e-mail. It made me feel madder than ever. This house was turning into some kind of torture chamber. If Harry wasn't yelling his head off, the twins were trapping me in their Magic Circles. And if Phoebe wasn't playing some evil trick on me, Alice was sulking or screaming about something or other. I'd never felt so completely hacked off with living here.

I came downstairs and looked in the living-room. Alice and Phoebe were watching a video, Alice sitting on the carpet, Phoebe lying on her stomach beside her, and Emma and Dad were talking quietly on the settee behind them.

Right, Phoebe, little do you know it, but you are for *it!*

'Dad?'

'Come and sit down, Ed. What have you been doing?'

'I've been reading my e-mails.'

'Oh yes?'

'Yes, there's one from a girl called Izzy who I can't stick. She's eleven years old and she's a friend of Alice's.'

Emma was looking at me with a puzzled frown on her face. Alice had stopped watching the video and turned round. Incredibly, Phoebe was the only person who didn't seem affected by what I was saying.

Just you wait, Phoebe.

'And it's funny because she sounds like she's replying to an e-mail from me. Only I've never sent her one, because I hate her guts, so why would I?'

Dad was looking puzzled too now. He nodded in agreement and leaned forwards.

Good! I'm getting everybody's attention.

I carried on – moving in for the kill.

'I looked in my *Sent Items* and found that Phoebe had sent an e-mail to this girl I hate, pretending to be me. So now the stupid girl thinks I really like her and she's invited herself over again on Saturday night.'

Emma's eyes were wide and Dad was throwing dangerous looks in Phoebe's direction. Phoebe still hadn't moved.

She will in a minute!

'She's just deliberately stirring things up and she's right out of order. Look. This is the piece of kiddish rubbish she sent.'

I flung the print-out of the e-mail at Dad, and flopped down on the carpet, my back to the settee. Dad and Emma held the paper between them as they read it, and even Alice jumped up on to the settee to have a look.

There was about twenty seconds of silence, then Dad let out this massive bellow of a laugh. I turned round in shock. I couldn't believe my ears. What was going on? Why wasn't Dad telling Phoebe she was grounded for six months with no pocket money? And now Emma was joining in too. They were sitting there, actually clutching each other as they rocked backwards and forwards, killing themselves laughing. Then Alice finished reading it and joined in the hilarious fun too.

Phoebe turned round and winked at Dad at that moment, and he bent forwards and ruffled her hair. He tried saying something to her, but it was impossible to understand because he was laughing so hysterically.

Something snapped inside me. I stood up, went over to the door and leaned against it.

Emma was the first one to realise that I was not happy. She tapped Dad on the arm and said 'Ssh!' Dad piped down slightly, but his eyes were watering from laughing so much. Alice kept chuckling quietly. Phoebe grinned at me.

'When you've finished . . .' I said in my iciest voice. Dad stopped then, and wiped his eyes with his hand. I spoke in hardly more than a whisper, '. . . you might like to know I'm going to live at Mum's from now on.'

Alice's chuckles froze. Emma clutched Dad's arm. Dad took a sharp intake of breath. I didn't look at Phoebe. I just turned and went back up to my room.

My heart was beating really fast. I'd shocked them into silence. Good! They'd be sorry they'd laughed now! I'd also shocked myself. I hadn't known I was going to say it. It had just come out. But it wasn't a bad idea. It'd certainly be an improvement on living at this place. Anything'd be better than this hell in four walls. I tapped in Mum's number.

'Hi Mum, it's me.'

'Hello, Edward. This is a nice surprise!'

'I've got something to ask you.'

There was a pause. '. . . Er . . . yes? . . . There's nothing wrong, is there?'

'I'm a bit fed up with living here . . .'

'Oh dear. Whatever's happened?'

'It's just too crowded, that's all. And sometimes I get stuck in the middle of things.'

'Oh dear.'

It was funny, but I suddenly felt like crying because she was all sympathetic and nice. Mum would never have laughed like Emma and Dad had done. She wouldn't find Phoebe's pathetic e-mail funny. In fact, she would have been furious with Phoebe for making trouble.

'I was wondering if I could live at your place . . .'

'Oh . . .'

'For a while.'

'Well . . . are you sure you've thought it all through? I mean, of course we'd love – well, obviously I'd have to talk to James about it, but I'm sure . . . Why don't you have another think about it? And in the meantime I'll have a word with James . . . and I'll have to speak to your father . . .'

Suddenly I desperately wanted to get off the phone. Mum wasn't exactly leaping around with excitement at the thought of me living at her place, was she?

'Yeah, OK, I'll phone you back tomorrow.'

I lay on my bed. My bones felt like they weighed about twenty tonnes. I should never have phoned. In fact I should never have said anything about wanting to live at Mum's in the first place. It's just that they made me feel like a total idiot. Especially Phoebe. She gets away with far too much.

Thinking about what she'd done to me and how they'd all laughed, made me more determined than ever to prove to them that I didn't have to put up with any of them if I didn't want to. I hoped they were all feeling really guilty down there. It served them right. In fact the more I thought about it, the more I was glad I said what I said. Mum was only sounding hesitant and confused because I'd given her a shock, coming out with it like that. She probably didn't know what to say because she knew there was Dad and James to talk to. But she was hardly going to turn me down, was she?

There was a knock on the door. 'Can I come in?' said Dad, in a sort of please-forgive-me voice.

Huh! He wasn't going to be let off *that* easily.

'What do you want?'

He came in and sat down on the bed.

'Just to say sorry. We were only laughing at Phoebe's ridiculous idea of a love letter. We didn't mean to upset you. We've told her off and she's gone to bed. She looked very sorry.'

'Big deal. She's a great actress – or hadn't you clicked?'

'I know she's an odd sort of child in many ways, Ed, but she's not malicious – just fun-loving.'

I spoke really slowly. 'You have no idea, Dad.'

'Emma and I are worried that you might be going to live at Mum's for the wrong reasons . . . I mean, you shouldn't regard it as a bolthole for when anything goes wrong. This little misunderstanding will clear up in no time at all, and then you might regret your decision . . .'

'*This little misunderstanding,* as you put it, isn't the only reason I want to live at Mum's.'

Dad looked surprised – kind of upset. 'Well . . . that's fine then. But why not just tell me what else is on your mind, because it might be something that can be sorted out easily . . .'

'You wouldn't understand.'

'Try me.'

I could feel my hackles rising, and I knew I was about to let him have all four barrels.

'This whole family is getting on my nerves. You've no idea what it's like having all these stepsisters. And they're all so weird – except Alice, who's giggly and stupid. And then there's Emma . . .'

Dad looked taken aback.

'Emma? Whatever has Emma done to upset you?'

'She's going back to work, isn't she?' My voice was sounding more and more sarcastic. 'A child minder'll be just great. Think *she'll* be able to keep Phoebe under control. And as for Harry – he'll just love it without his mother around.' Dad was frowning at the carpet. I decided to give him something to frown about, to pay him back for laughing at me. He's never taken me seriously. 'Anyway I've arranged it now. Mum's really happy. And so am I.'

Just before I rolled over and sat on the other side of my bed with my back to him, I saw the look in his eyes. I'd hurt him. Good.

13 TOO LATE!

When I woke up the following morning it felt like something was wrong. Then I remembered what had happened the night before. Everything was different. I was going to live at Mum's. My eyes flew open but I shut them again quickly and sighed.

I didn't want to go and live at Mum's. I only had to think about the white carpet and the white towel and the stupid way James spoke to Zac to remind myself that I'd rather live in my headteacher's office.

But I was stuck with it now, so I'd better get

used to the idea. Think of the positives. Right. It's not *that* far from here. I'll still be going to the same school and everything – just coming from the opposite direction. Shane and Tom and Josh will still be my mates. And best of all, I'll never have anyone playing stupid tricks on me, or catching me up in their silly pretends, or making me chase after spiders. There'll be no Reggae Rattlesnake, no screams, no stupid giggles, no nasty Phoebe-type surprises and no Izzy. But there'd also be no Dad . . . So what? He was nearly always at work, so I wouldn't miss *him* . . . And no Emma. Well, she was about to go back to work too. So it wouldn't make any difference where I lived as far as those two were concerned.

At breakfast time everyone was quiet, even Harry. Dad had gone to work. I sat there munching my toast, feeling all eyes on me.

'We're going to tell Izzy she can't come on

Saturday,' said Alice quietly after several minutes' silence.

'Unless you want to tell her yourself,' said Emma quickly.

'No way am I speaking to *her*,' I said without looking up.

'You won't be troubled with her again, Ed. Alice doesn't even particularly like her.'

There was another silence. It was weird all these silences in this house. It wasn't right.

'Did you just say that about living at your mum's because you were in a temper, Ed?' asked Alice quietly. 'I mean, you're not really going to leave us, are you?'

I saw Emma shake her head quickly at Alice, as if to tell her to shut up. If Alice thought she could win me round that easily she had another think coming.

'Course I am.'

'Why?'

'I'll get some peace there.'

Alice looked at Emma and Emma started briskly clearing plates away. The twins looked at each other and started mouthing something or other that I couldn't follow. It was probably in some private language of theirs.

'Can we get down?' asked Amy.

'Go and wash your hands, both of you,' said Emma.

As I was extracting Harry's sticky fingers from my hair a moment later, the phone rang. I went to answer it and it was Mum.

'Hello, Edward. Good news. James and I have had a chat, and of course you must come and live here if that's what you want . . . Oops-a-dearie! Sorry, Edward, Zac's just tugging at my earring . . . Ow! Ouch! Zac, that hurt. Zacky, you are such a little pickle!'

I closed my eyes. Any second now she's going to break into the Voice.

'Yes he is! He's a pickle!'

I'd forgotten how bad it sounded – the Voice.

Mum seemed to have forgotten something too – that I was hanging on the other end of the line. She was still talking to Zac.

'What are you? Hm? You're a pickle!'

'Mum?'

'Yes, sorry, Edward. Where were we? Oh yes, Dad phoned me from work. He suggested you move in at the weekend. What about that?'

'Fine.'

I was saying 'fine' but I wasn't feeling it, and when I'd rung off I felt it even less. Dad had suggested when I should go. Maybe he's been secretly wanting me to go for ages, I thought. After all, there are so many of us living here, and I don't really fit in because I'm the oldest, and I'm also the only who's got nothing to do with Emma – I mean, I'm not a blood relation.

Right. That's settled then. I'm going to live at Mum's. I feel terrible.

Wonder what the twins are up to. I went

outside. They were in their hut-house. I could hear them through the wooden walls.

'I asked Mummy for the number. We'll have to practise sounding like proper grown-ups.'

'Yes, because this is very important.'

'Yes.'

For once they weren't playing at pretends. It sounded like they were actually having a serious conversation. I wandered down the drive. Phoebe was in her tree-house, I could see her shadow through the sheet. She was keeping perfectly still.

'I know you know I know you're here, you know, Ed.'

What?

'It's dangerous up there,' I remarked.

'I don't care.' *Typical. That kid would never change.* 'It's my fault you're going to live at your mum's, isn't it?'

'Partly.'

She didn't say anything after that, so I went

back in the house and upstairs. Alice was sitting outside her bedroom door.

'What are you doing?' I said.

'I can't go in.'

'Why?'

'There's a spider by the curtain.'

I sighed. 'So you're waiting for me to come and move it?'

'No.'

'Right. OK, so you're trying to get rid of it by thought transference?'

'No. I just don't want to go inside.'

'Look, Alice, do you want me to move it? Because if you do, you've only got to ask.'

'If I ask, will it make you want to leave us even more?'

'It's all decided. I'm leaving,' I told her as I went in her room and looked round for the spider.

It didn't a take a minute to find it. I managed to scoop it up and was about to chuck it out of the window when Alice said, 'I'll try and hold it, if you want.'

Her voice was very shaky and it was obvious she was scared out of her mind.

'It's OK, it's quite big. You ought to start with a smaller one,' I said.

Then I chucked it out and went into my own room. My stomach was grinding round like a concrete mixer. I wasn't sure why. It was something to do with the way Alice's voice had sounded when she'd said she'd hold the spider. She was trying to please me!

My mobile started ringing. I pressed the green button.

'Hello.'

'This is Ed Carlisle's fairy godmother.'

It was Amy. She was trying to make herself sound grown-up and important. I could hear the effort in her voice. So *this* was what they'd been discussing in their hut-house. But why phone me?

And then as I listened I realised that they really thought I'd be taken in by them.

'I am phoning with a very important new law. From now on, Ed Carlisle will get peace because no one is allowed to pester him ever again. That is an order. No one will mess up Ed's games or say a certain name, what is called Izzy.'

There was a scuffle, then Lucy's voice came on the line, putting on the same voice. 'And everyone will be kind to Ed Carlisle because the fairy godmother is in charge. Also, Ed must stay and live in this house. It is a special law of the fairy godmother.'

There were a few noises and a whisper before they disconnected. It was the whisper that got my stomach churning again.

'He'll stay here now.'

I closed my eyes. Alice and the twins were desperately trying to show me that they wanted me to stay. But I can't. I've told everyone I'm going. I'll look a right twit if I change my mind. The arrangements have been made. There's no going back.

14 WHERE IS SHE?

By Saturday morning I felt dizzy from thinking so much. I'd been round to Josh's two days before and told him what I was going to do. He thought I was off my rocker at first, but when I went on about what it was like having to put up with all my stepsisters, he said he could understand why I wanted to live at Mum's.

'So will you come and visit your dad and everyone?' he'd asked.

' 'Spose.'

I'd never thought of that. It seemed pretty weird.

Shane had come round yesterday and when he'd been here a couple of hours, I'd told him about the big decision.

'I don't get you, Ed.'

'That's because you don't know how bad my sisters can be. And then there's Harry. He's a pain at times. And Emma – she's getting a job. It won't be the same with her working. I'll be landed with the others much more.'

'Perhaps it's just part-time or something.'

'Oh yeah! *Very* likely. I thought you'd be on my side.'

'What's it matter what I think? You'll be at your mum's.'

'So? We'll see each other at school.'

He'd shrugged and that was the end of the conversation. Then when he'd gone later, I felt that awful grinding thing again. I was getting sick of it.

In the evening Tom had phoned.

'I thought you were still on holiday.'

'We came back early.'

'Why?'

'Rain.'

Good old Tom. He hadn't changed.

'Do you want to come over tomorrow morning?' I asked.

'Can't. Afternoon?'

'Sorry. I'm moving to Mum's.'

'Moving? What – for good?'

'Yeah.'

There was a long silence. I knew why. It was because Tom had got loads of questions he wanted to ask me, but being Tom, he couldn't ask them, especially not on the phone, so he was hanging on waiting for me to start explaining. He could forget that.

Then he spoke. Just two words.

'You doughnut!'

'Oh cheers, Tom.' There was a silence. 'You can get me on my mobile.'

He grunted, I said we could get together the

next week, he grunted again, then we rang off.

So the time had almost come. I was in my room, packing. I wasn't allowed to take my spinning chair or my computer desk. Not because Dad and Emma wouldn't let me. It was Mum. She'd told me on the phone that the kind of stuff we'd got at home wouldn't suit their new house.

It was going to take two trips in the car to take everything over. Emma and Dad were helping me. Alice was hovering nearby. Phoebe and the twins were keeping an eye on Harry in the playroom.

My room was looking barer and barer. The walls had got dark rectangles on them where I'd taken my posters down. There were dusty patches on the top of my chest of drawers instead of all my stuff. The carpet was faded and covered in bits of fluff and dirt except for the place where the rug had been.

'So *that's* where your report got to!' said

Emma, picking up a dusty envelope which had appeared on the carpet when Dad started to move the computer desk.

She was tapping it against her other hand and giving me a mock telling-off sort of look. It was weird but I suddenly wished she *would* tell me off. In fact I wanted Dad to open it and see how badly I'd done at school last year, and blow a fuse. But all he said was, 'Oh well, water under the bridge now.'

It felt as though there was a massive weight in my ribcage making my whole body heavy and slow.

'We've got a letter from Phoebe!' said Lucy, crashing into the room so the door banged hard against the wall. 'Where's your caterpillar?' she added, because it was my draught-excluder caterpillar which used to stop the door hitting the wall.

'Packed,' I told her.

'We haven't got time for letters from Phoebe,'

said Dad. 'I hope she's keeping an eye on Harry,' he added, seeing Amy come in and stare round with big horrified eyes.

'You've got to read it,' said Amy, dragging her eyes from the bare walls.

'Later,' said Emma. 'She *is* with Harry though, isn't she?'

The twins looked at each other.

'Don't tell me you've all three gone off and left him?'

'We put him in his playpen before Phoebe went.'

'Went where?'

'You've got to read the letter.'

Emma ripped open the envelope and started reading aloud. The twins both covered their eyes for some unknown reason and Alice sat cross-legged on the floor.

> '*Dear Mum and Gordon,*
> *Ed is going because of me. Alice says he*

doesn't mind so much about her spider fear any more, and also she's told him that Izzy isn't coming to our house again, so it isn't because of that. The twins say it's not their fault because they've promised not to pester him any more. But he's still going, and Harry is too little to make anyone cross, so it must be because of me. I know you are both sad because I've heard you talking about it when I've listened outside your bedroom door after bed time. I have run away now, so you can tell Ed that it is all right for him to stay. I have got my toothbrush and some spare clothes in my P.E. bag.

Love from Phoebe.

'Omigod!' said Emma.

I flopped on to the bed, feeling suddenly weak.

'When did she go?' Dad asked the twins

urgently. Then because they didn't answer straight away, he shouted it. 'When did she go? Think!'

'She said we had to wait until the clock said 11 dot dot 30, before we came to tell you.'

'And can you remember what the time was when she said that?'

They screwed up their faces and looked up at the ceiling as if it might be written there. Eventually Amy said, '11 dot dot 25.'

'Only five minutes ago,' Dad said to Emma. 'She can't have gone far.' Then he turned to me, as if he suddenly realised that he'd forgotten something very important. He put his hands on my shoulders. 'It's not your fault, Ed. Phoebe gets strange ideas in her head. We all know that.'

I felt like crying then. My throat was in agony because I was trying so hard to stop myself.

'It *is* my fault. She asked me if she was the

reason I was going and I said "partly". So now she thinks it can't be because of Alice and the twins, so it must be all because of her.'

I couldn't speak any more. Emma put her arm round me.

'It's only because she thinks such a lot of you, Ed.'

'It's not. It's because she's sorry for you and Dad. That's what she said.'

'She *is* sorry for us, I'm sure, but she cares about you more than anyone in this family.'

I couldn't believe what I was hearing. Phoebe devoted her life to trying to get me into trouble.

'Emma's right,' said Dad. 'Why do you think she follows you around all over the place and copies everything you do, and tries to impress you all the time?'

'And do you know what she said to me when we got cross about the e-mail she sent to Izzy?' Emma went on. I shrugged as though I didn't care, but really I was dying to know. 'She said,

"I thought Ed would think it was really clever of me." You see, she's so desperate for you to think she's bright and witty, it never even occurred to her that you'd be cross. She just thought you'd take it as a joke.'

'We've got to find her,' said Dad. 'I'll take the car and the mobile so we can keep in touch.'

'OK, maybe I ought to phone Simon . . .'

'She'd never go to Dad's, Mum,' said Alice. 'It's miles away.'

'No . . . you're right. I'm not thinking straight. I'll phone a couple of her friends' parents. Then I'll put Harry in his buggy . . .' Emma set off after Dad, calling instructions over her shoulder. 'You can search the house and garden in case she's hiding, you lot. Make sure Alice and the twins don't go out of the drive, Ed.'

Alice and the twins went crashing off and I was left alone in my room. I started thinking about what Emma and Dad had said about Phoebe. I'd thought she only followed me round to annoy me, not because she wanted to be with me. And then there was the bit about the e-mail. Did she really do it because she wanted me to think she was clever? The kid had got more slates missing than the roof of the hut-house.

I went down into the living-room and started rifling through the wastepaper bin. There at the bottom was the crumpled up print-out of Phoebe's e-mail. I read through it, imagining her sitting there at my computer, grinning to herself. Before I knew it I was laughing. I had to hand it to her, it was a wicked idea.

I came back to earth with a jolt. Phoebe was missing. Anything could have happened to her. She'd been gone ten minutes now. What the hell was I doing? I had to help find her. Where would she have gone? Think, Ed. Think!

15 BACK TO NORMAL

I knew where Phoebe was. It was obvious.

'I'll go and get her,' I called to Emma as I rushed to the back door.

'What? You know where she is?'

'Yup.'

'I'll come too!'

'It's OK . . . I'll be faster on my own.'

'Go on then . . . I'll phone your dad.' I heard the triumph in her voice as I shot out of the house. 'I knew you'd be the one to suss where she was!'

* * *

I arrived at the tree in Broomleigh Lane. This was where we'd been standing when she'd asked me if I wanted to see her hiding place. It must be somewhere very close by. I looked round. There was a fence on one side of the path and a hedge on the other. I investigated the bottom of the hedge but it would have been impossible to crawl through. I stood there, racking my brains.

Then it came to me. Of course – Phoebe and trees. She was obsessed with climbing them – like the one at the bottom of our drive. I stood by the trunk of the tree but didn't look up.

'Big problem, Phoebe,' I said.

No answer.

'You see, I've decided not to go to Mum's because when I got thinking about it, I realised I'd probably be pretty miserable away from everyone . . .'

Still no answer.

'Trouble is, I don't think I'll be happy at Dad's either, unless you're there . . . because you're the one who's most like me out of the whole family, you see . . .'

A P.E. bag dropped at my feet.

'Stay there!' came Phoebe's voice from above.

'What?'

'Just stay there . . . and get ready . . . Geronimo!'

She came like a bullet out of the tree and landed on my back. Somehow I managed not to collapse.

'That was good, wasn't it, Ed?'

I was on the point of telling her it was dangerous and stupid, not good, when I remembered what Emma had said.

'Yeah, pretty good. Not as good as that daft e-mail, though. That was a stroke of genius. It might have been an idea to check I did actually fancy the girl first, but still . . .'

She didn't laugh and I couldn't see her face, but it was great to imagine her grinning away under that baseball cap.

I jogged all the way home with Phoebe on my back. As we rounded the bend just before the end of our drive, there they all were. Harry started clapping wildly, the twins jumped up and down, Alice came running to meet us, and Emma and Dad just stood there smiling.

We all walked back up the drive to the house together, Emma and Dad on either side of me. Phoebe had jumped down and was carrying Harry.

'What about Mum?' I said to Dad. 'Can you phone her and explain?'

Dad coughed and looked a bit embarrassed. 'I already have done. It's all un-arranged.'

'Wasn't she cross?'

'Nah. I just mentioned all the mugs of half-finished tea and the mouldy old bits of cheese sandwiches we found lying around in your room, and she sounded quite relieved actually.'

I laughed and wondered how the conversation had really gone.

'So now we've got to get your room back to normal,' said Emma. She had a thoughtful look in her eye. 'Perhaps I might take the opportunity to redecorate it . . .'

'You won't have time, will you?' I said a bit more snappily than I'd meant to.

'Time?'

I tried not to sound too sulky, but it was like something jarring inside me. 'Because of your job.'

'Oh, that . . . I'm not doing that after all. It was only part-time, but the hours weren't really going to . . . fit in . . . with Harry.'

I looked at Dad, trying to get a clue from his face, but he wasn't giving anything away. I guessed I'd never know whether she'd done that because of me.

'I'll help you redecorate,' I said, hoping she was getting the message that I was glad she wasn't taking the job.

'Great!'

She smiled right at me. She'd got the message loud and clear.

'Can we do it later though? There's something I want to get in town first.'

'Can I come?' Phoebe asked.

'Suppose so,' I said, twisting her cap the right way round. 'You'll only follow me otherwise.'

'Cool!' she said, grinning up at me as though she hadn't expected me to let her come.

And then I knew for sure that Emma and Dad were right. Phoebe really *did* want to be with me.

'What are you going to get in town?' she asked as we set off.

'Oh, just some old thing for my stepsister. What's it called? Oh yeah – Gritty Grace.'

There was a silence, then she suddenly held my hand.

'Thanks, bruv!' she breathed.

PARENTS BEHAVING BADLY

1 FAMILIES OUT OF STEP

'OK, pipe down you lot!' said Mrs Waghorn, standing up at the front of the coach for about the tenth time.

'It's because we're all in a good mood, Miss,' said Chris Carter, the year nine mouthpiece.

The boys at the back all jeered, but jokingly. They liked Chris. He always spoke his mind.

'Yeah, you should be flattered, Miss. It's you who put us in a good mood.'

'Just sit down and be quiet for the last ten minutes. You say I've made *you* happy – well, now make *me* happy.'

We were on our way back from a really brilliant play. It was a school outing for years eight and nine. The theatre company we'd just seen only ever did performances for schools, especially to help students understand Shakespeare. Even the loud boys like Chris and Sean really enjoyed it.

I loved the whole outing because my stepsister Rachel and I got to sit next to each other on the coach there and back. She's in year eight and I'm in year nine, though our birthdays aren't that far apart.

'Oi, Hannah! Isn't that your brother?' Chris asked me.

The coach had stopped at the lights. I rubbed the window with my hand because it was all steamed up. Craig was walking on the opposite pavement a little way ahead.

Rachel leaned over me and peered out too. 'He's right, it *is* Craig. What's he doing, Han?'

'Haven't a clue,' I said.

She lowered her voice. 'Is he still acting

strange?' I nodded. 'Poor Han.'

'Poor, pathetic parents more like.'

'What are you two whispering about?' asked Katie, one of my best friends in year nine, draping her arms over our seat from behind.

'Nothing interesting,' said Rachel.

We'd pulled away from the lights and were catching up with Craig. I knocked on the window to attract his attention, then half the coach joined in.

'Craig!' called Naomi, my other best friend in year nine.

'Girls at the back, less noise!' said Mrs Waghorn. 'You're still representing the school, you know.'

'Yes, shut up, girls!' said Chris, putting on a teacherly voice. 'Learn some decent manners like us boys!'

All the boys laughed, and Craig happened to glance up at that moment and catch sight of me. He hardly smiled at all.

'Your brother doesn't look too happy. Have you been upsetting him, Hannah?' asked Chris, grinning all over his face.

'Shut up, Chris,' said Rachel. 'You wouldn't understand a family problem if you had three years' private coaching on the subject.'

I knew Rachel would tell Chris where to get off. We always stick up for each other because we're not only stepsisters, we're best friends too.

As we approached the school, people started dragging their bags down from the luggage racks.

'Who's picking you up?' Rachel asked me, her eyes all sympathetic.

'Mum.'

'What time's Dad coming home?'

'Usual, I think.'

'Give me a ring if things get bad.'

'Yeah. Thanks.'

Rachel is the only person who understands

what it's like at home these days. We've known each other since she was six and I was seven. That's when her dad (Tony) left her mum, because he'd fallen in love with *my* mum. Mum and Craig and I had been living on our own for about a year before that, because my real dad left Mum and went to Scotland.

It seems so long ago now, but Dad had been spending more and more time in Scotland on business, and finally he decided to move up there for good. Mum didn't want to go with him and because I was quite young at the time I couldn't work out why. It turned out that he had a girlfriend. It was horrible just before he went, but it was a relief when he'd actually gone. Mum seemed happier, and I didn't miss him because I'd got so used to him being away.

Lots of people think it's weird because Rachel's dad is my stepdad, but Rachel and I are really fine with it. We've both got a mum and a stepdad to live with, and it makes things even better that we're stepsisters.

The problem is our mums. They don't speak to each other if they can possibly help it, because they can't stand each other. It can be quite embarrassing and awkward for Rachel and me at times, even though we're used to it now. Sometimes we feel like wringing our mothers' necks and telling them to grow up, but we've found it best not to say anything if we don't want to get screamed at.

When Tony first moved in with us, there were massive arguments on the phone between Rachel's mum and him. Since then each set of parents has tried to pretend the other doesn't exist. Our mums used to try and keep us apart. Rachel's mum, Tigs, didn't want her daughter in the same house as Mum because she was so jealous of her, especially when Mum and Tony got married. And Mum's never been happy about Tigs and her new husband, Simon, living so close. She hates it when Tony has to get in touch with Tigs about anything to do with Rachel or Susannah, his other daughter. I can tell she wishes that Rachel and I weren't best friends, but she knows after all these years that she can't stop us.

But these last few months everything's worse than ever because things have started to go wrong between Mum and Tony. If Tony ever left us I'd be gutted because he's just like a proper dad to me and Craig. But the arguments between him and Mum are getting worse. Sometimes it's like they hate each other's guts.

The coach swung into the school car park, and I saw Mum's car straight away. When I looked carefully I could also see her face. She was pressing her fingertips against her lips and staring straight ahead blankly. This was her usual expression these days.

I said 'bye to everyone then got in the car.

'So. Was it good?'

Mum's face came to life with a big bright

smile. It reminded me of the moment when the Prince kisses the Sleeping Beauty and she wakes up.

'Yeah, excellent. Even Chris Carter liked it.'

'Wow! It *must* have been good!'

'I'm starving.'

'Spag bol tonight.'

I wanted to know if Tony was going to eat with us, or if he was going to be late back from work again, but I didn't dare even say his name. It would only make Mum go tense and tight-lipped. That's how all the bad stuff started with my real dad. Even when he wasn't actually away, he kept on being late home from work.

To make matters worse, Craig is changing. He and I used to talk to each other about all sorts of stuff, but if I try to talk now, he just grunts out a reply. So I've given up. I know he hates it when Mum and Tony are arguing, but it's almost as if he's taking it out on me.

* * *

Tony wasn't late, but we didn't all eat together. He and Craig ate their spag bol in the kitchen, while Mum and I went into the living-room and watched telly. Craig acts practically normally when he and Tony are together, as long as Mum isn't in the same room. They laugh and joke as though they don't have a care in the world. But the moment Mum comes in, Craig suddenly goes all bolshie.

'I'll take the plates through,' I said during the adverts.

Mum just nodded. Her face had got that marble look on it, and I wondered if she'd actually taken in any of the programme, or if she'd just been staring at the screen, wrapped up in her own thoughts, seeing nothing except the pictures inside her head.

In the kitchen Craig and Tony were playing a game on their mobile phones. Tony didn't even know he'd got any games on his phone until Craig showed him. And now he's obsessed. The two of them sit there, staring at their tiny little screens and trying to get a higher score than the other one.

'Can you show me how to play?' I asked, seeing them having such a good time.

'Sssh!' said Craig, his thumbs tapping away.

I loaded the plates in the dishwasher while they finished.

'Top score! Six hundred!' yelled Tony, as his phone rang a bright little tune to celebrate. 'What did you get?'

'Four hundred and fifty,' said Craig, looking hacked off.

'That makes it three–two, I believe!'

'Oh thanks, Hannah,' Craig said sarcastically to me.

'What? I didn't do anything.'

'You made me lose concentration.'

'So-*rry*!'

'Yeah, right. Tony's the overall winner now.'

'Let me have a go, Craig,' I begged.

'You'll never beat the champ,' swaggered Tony.

And that was when Mum came into the kitchen.

Something instantly changed. We might as well have pumped in ice-cold air. It was horrible, just like it always was these days.

'I'm off to Josh's,' Craig said, scraping his chair as he got up.

'See you later,' said Tony, trying to keep his voice light, but failing.

Craig grunted. He's nearly sixteen. He can escape – lucky thing. I'm only thirteen, so it's a bit more difficult.

'I've got homework,' I mumbled as I got up.

I waited outside the kitchen door to hear what they'd say, even though I knew it was a stupid thing to do because I'd only get upset. It's horrible when you hear two people you love having an argument.

'They both take off like frightened animals

the moment we're in the same room,' said Mum.

She sounded tired and sad.

Then Tony spoke. 'We were perfectly OK till *you* came in.'

'Are you saying it's my fault?'

'I'm just saying we were perfectly OK till you came in.'

The phone rang. Tony answered it.

'Hello . . . Hello, love. How're you doing?'

It was either Susannah or Rachel. These days, apart from me, the only people he talks to in that affectionate tone of voice are his real daughters. Let's hope it was Rachel. I felt like a chat.

Hang on a sec . . . what am I saying? If it is Rachel, I'm going to get caught eavesdropping outside the kitchen door at any second!

I rushed upstairs in the nick of time.

'Hannah . . . phone. It's Rachel,' called Tony.

'I'll take it up here.'

Getting the phone from Mum and Tony's room, I went into my own room and lay on the bed.

'Hi, Han. Guess what . . . Mum's found this conditioner that's supposed to straighten your hair. You leave it on for twenty minutes and keep combing and combing your hair the whole time it's on. I'm doing it now!'

It was always great to hear Rachel's voice. Even when I've been with her loads during the day, like today, we never run out of things to say. Rachel's got a thing about her curly hair. She says she'd give anything to have straight hair like mine. But the trouble with mine is that it's too fine. The only reason I've grown it nearly to my waist is because if I had it any shorter, it'd look like I'd hardly *got* any hair.

'Sounds great, Rach! Can't wait to see it tomorrow!'

'Are things really bad, Han?'

I didn't think I'd shown my feelings in my

voice, but Rachel knows me so well, she can tell if anything's wrong, even when I try to cover it up.

'You're not kidding. Mum walked into the room and the atmosphere froze over, then when they tried speaking to each other there was an instant argument. Can you come round?'

'I'll ask. Expect me if you see me.'

'OK.'

We often used those words – *expect me if you see me* – at the end of our phone calls. Basically, it means *I'll be allowed to come over if Mum's in a good mood*. I know it's strange that I live with Rachel's dad, but most of the time it feels completely normal. Just occasionally it hits me though – like now. My best friend is sympathising with me about *my* problem living with *her* dad. How weird is *that*? I know she's got her own stepdad, but in a way that just makes it even stranger, because *his* children live with someone else's dad . . . And so it goes on. It's one great long chain of families, all out of step with each other.

Collect the links in the step-chain . . .

 1. To see her dad Sarah has to stay with the woman who wrecked her family. Will she do it? Find out in *One Mum Too Many!*

 2. Ollie thinks a holiday with girls will be a nightmare. And it is, because he's fallen for his stepsister. Can it get any worse? Find out in *You Can't Fancy Your Stepsister*

3. Lissie's half-sister is a spoilt brat, but her mum thinks she's adorable. Can Lissie make her see what's really going on? Find out in *She's No Angel*

 4. Becca's mum describes her boyfriend's daughter as perfect in every way. Can Becca bear to meet her? Find out in *Too Good To Be True*

 6. Hannah and Rachel are stepsisters. They're also best friends. What will happen to them if their parents split up? Find out in *Parents Behaving Badly*